JOSHUA
IN A TROUBLED WORLD

JOSHUA

IN A TROUBLED WORLD

Joseph F. Girzone

IMAGE BOOKS DOUBLEDAY

New York London Toronto Sydney Auckland

AN IMAGE BOOK
PUBLISHED BY DOUBLEDAY
a division of Random House, Inc.

IMAGE, DOUBLEDAY, and the portrayal of a deer drinking from a stream
are registered trademarks of Random House, Inc.

Book design by Elizabeth Rendfleisch

Library of Congress Cataloging-in-Publication Data
Girzone, Joseph F.
Joshua in a troubled world / Joseph F. Girzone.— 1st ed.
p. cm.
(alk. paper)
1. Joshua (Fictitious character)—Fiction. 2. International relations—Fiction.
3. Second Advent—Fiction. I. Title.
PS3557.I77J646 2005

813'.54—dc22   2004055116

ISBN-13: 978-0-385-51183-4
ISBN-10: 0-385-51183-3

July 2006

First Image Edition

1 3 5 7 9 10 8 6 4 2

AN OLD MAN WAS KNEELING AT HIS BEDSIDE, CRYING, PRAY-
ing, reaching out to the heavens: "Time of fear, time of shame,
time of danger, time of hatred all around. Desperation, helpless-
ness across the world. Christians terrorize Christians. Jews and
Arabs fear each other's vengeful hatred. War against terror de-
stroys innocent lives, collateral damage, friendly fire, sanitizing
the guilt. Leaders applaud injustice in their friends in exchange
for votes, increasing vengeance from their enemies, multiplying
our enemies. Pontius Pilate is still alive and well, though now a
Christian; and Jesus, in the least of our brothers and sisters, is
sold and crucified not once, but daily—not for silver, but for
votes dripping with blood. Is there no savior for our hopeless
world? Lord, can you save us a second time, this time from ourselves? Concerned with political interests, our leaders have lost
the trust of honest people to mediate a just and lasting peace.
They mouth religion but have no honest trust in the divine.
They cannot be the savior; they are the problem. In their

mouths they say, 'In God we trust.' But their hearts insist, 'In God we *cannot* trust. We will be God. We will save the world. We will rid the world of evil.' What atheists express in words, our leaders second by their actions."

That may have been the prayer of an old man on the threshold of another world, but it clearly represents the feelings of people across the world. Some have known nothing but this terror since the day they were born, especially those driven from their homes for others to occupy. For others it is a new experience, like a nightmare in full daylight.

The troubles of our world have far exceeded the ability of the human mind to comprehend, which paralyzes our ability to solve them. Is there no one to save us, this time from ourselves?

PENNSYLVANIA AVENUE WAS FLOWING WITH PEDESTRI-
ans crisscrossing in every direction like a floating colony
of ants. Busy and confusing as it was to the casual eye, one man
in that vast crowd stood out. Calm, detached from all around
him, he walked with determination. Under ordinary circumstances he would appear as just different, but in the current
heavy atmosphere of political paranoia, the man's Middle Eastern appearance set him apart as possibly sinister. Though poorly
dressed, he did not seem like a homeless beggar. His resolute
gaze indicated he was a man with a purpose. What kind of purpose? Who was he? Where was he from? What was he doing at
this particular time in Washington, D.C.? What made him stand
out was his total lack of interest in the sights. Ordinary visitors
gawked in every direction, unwilling to miss anything. This
man appeared disinterested in everything around him. His de-
tachment caused wonder and aroused suspicion in anyone
whose concern was the security of the area. As the stranger

walked closer and closer to the White House, he was approached by two neatly dressed men who asked for his identification. Of course, Joshua had none.

"I think you better come with us," one of them said, flashing his badge as a government agent.

"Why, what have I done?" Joshua asked with a calm, confused look.

"Never mind! Just come with us and don't give us any trouble."

As the three walked along, the younger of the two asked Joshua how long he had been in Washington. "I just arrived," was the quick reply.

"Where did you come from?" was the next question.

Joshua's vague response told them nothing, increasing their suspicion. A black Ford pulled up along the curb. The driver emerged and opened the rear door. The two men directed Joshua to get in, then took their places on either side of him as the car sped off down the street to an FBI office.

Dan Halloran had been working for the Bureau for a little over a year, having finished his law degree at Georgetown just a few months before. His father had been in the military, spending his last years as a briefing officer at the Pentagon, so they had connections enough to find good positions for family members. Dan was dedicated to his new assignment of monitoring approaches to the White House. Like his father, he was clean-cut, rigid, seeing life in black and white, with no possibility of shades in between. His partner, Tom Clark, was older. He had been an agent for over ten years and was slightly more casual in the performance of his assigned duties, at least as casual as the agency's discipline would allow.

Sitting on one side of the table with Joshua sitting across from them, the two men interrogated him.

"You said your name was Joshua?" Dan Halloran asked him.

"Yes."

"What is your last name?" the agent continued.

"I rarely use my last name," Joshua replied.

"I don't care whether you use it or not. What is it?"

"Ben-Youssef."

"Is that Palestinian?" Tom Clark asked him.

"No, the name is Hebrew."

"Hebrew? Sounds Arabic to me. Are you an American citizen?"

"I belong here, if that is what you are asking."

"Answer the question," Dan insisted. "Are you an American? Do you have an American passport?"

"I never needed one."

"What is your nationality?" Dan asked impatiently, realizing this was not going to be an easy day.

"I have no nationality. I am a member of every family."

"Then you're an illegal alien?"

"That is your term. I am not illegal, nor am I here illegally. I have been here long before you were born."

"Are you just being difficult? Or are you hiding something?" Tom interjected.

"I am hiding nothing. You are the ones who picked me off the street although I had done nothing wrong and have no intention of doing harm to anyone. Why do you suspect me? Because I am poor? Because I look like someone you prejudge to be evil? If I have done nothing wrong, then why do you interrogate me? You are the ones who are doing what is unjust, profiling people because of the way they look and the clothes they wear. Fear does terrible things to people, pushing ordinarily normal people into doing things that would be unthinkable in ordinary times. I am surprised and saddened that this could happen in this beautiful country."

"Since you cannot prove your citizenship, you *must* be here illegally," Dan continued with mounting frustration.

"How many people walking down Pennsylvania Avenue carry with them proof of citizenship? I am not alien to America. I have always been here, and I will always be here. Unless you can prove that I am an illegal alien, I ask that you release me."

Realizing that they were getting nowhere and that the man was right in saying they had no legal cause to hold him, they fingerprinted him, took his name, declined to demand his Social Security number, since it would be futile anyway, and released him. However, for the whole period of Joshua's stay, he was shadowed everywhere he went. His every movement was watched and recorded, his every word written down.

Joshua continued wandering through the city, casually enjoying the sights as he walked along, but without appearing to be a tourist stretching his neck to miss nothing. His real purpose was to meet certain individuals, and even though he had been sidetracked by his arrest, he knew just where he had to be and at precisely what times he should be there. Even this apparently unforeseen incident had been taken into consideration.

Joshua's encounter with the police plainly evidenced the threatening atmosphere pervading the country. It was not always like that, only during times of national stress when people's basic human rights are often trampled, and the lives of so many innocent people are destroyed, and their reputations and businesses are ruined by the all-pervasive paranoia. Certain government officials will have their way for a few years, then the people come to their senses and realize they have been blinded by zealots whose obsession threatens the rights of everyone. Then the life of the nation drifts back to normal. Hopefully this current obsession would also pass before it did more damage to people than the evil it was trying to prevent.

Continuing his walk around the city, Joshua turned up North Capitol, stopping at St. Aloysius Gonzaga, an old Jesuit church in the heart of the city. Knowing he was being followed, he gave no heed, for he had a much better surveillance system that made it possible for him to be always a giant step ahead of them. After entering the church, he looked around and spotted a man halfway up the middle aisle. He was kneeling with bowed head, deep in prayer. Joshua approached and tapped him on the shoulder. Startled, the man turned and looked up.

"Yes, what do you want?" the man asked in a deep, brusque voice.

"I have come to answer your prayer," Joshua replied.

"How do you know what I was praying for?"

"You are praying for your son. You are worried about him because of the company he has been keeping lately."

"What is it you have to tell me? But, first of all, who are you? What is your name?"

"My name is Joshua. And I know your son well. He is a good boy, and you are afraid that he is mixed up in something that will bring him harm and will bring shame upon your family. You are afraid something terrible is going to happen to him."

"How do you know all these things? I have never told a soul."

"I understand. But I tell you your son is protected from above. Nothing evil will befall him. He is disturbed over the plight of your people and wants to do something heroic, but he has innocently approached the wrong people."

"Sir, you are right. I know what you are saying. That is

why I am so afraid. I have heard of those people. I grew up with some of them, but they are nothing like our family. We are a good, honest people, and hardworking. My son has always been a good boy. I pray to God that nothing will happen to him."

The man extended his hand to Joshua. "My name is Benyamin. I came here years ago to escape trouble in my country. Bethlehem, where I lived, was supposed to be a city of peace, but we have never known a day of peace. I thought that if I brought my family here, we would find peace. For a while we did, but now it is all turning sour, and I am afraid things will get worse. People follow us because we look suspicious and our names are strange, and because we came from Palestine."

"Benyamin, do not worry! I know you well. You and your family are people of deep faith. God has something very special for your son to do. Do not worry about him! God has answered your prayers. Your son will be safe."

"How do you know?" the man asked.

"I know. Trust me. Go home and tell your wife to be at peace. All will be well with your son."

"I don't know who you are, sir, or how you know, but you already make me feel at peace," the man said as tears began to flow down his cheeks.

As Joshua turned to leave the church, the man continued his prayers, this time thanking God for all His goodness.

As soon as Joshua stepped outside, he noticed the two agents casually watching from across the street. It brought back memories of days of old, when scribes and Pharisees and their henchmen followed him everywhere he went, jotting notes, cataloging his every move and everything he said and the names of the people close to him. He knew that this would be even more complicated because of the modern sophisticated eavesdropping equipment that made it possible for spies to snoop almost totally undetected. He would have to be careful, "simple as a dove, sly as a fox." Yet it really did not trouble him; he was going to have fun, since he knew his own eavesdropping abilities were far superior to their electronic gadgets. He would have no trouble outfoxing them.

As Joshua continued his walk up North Capitol, he encountered a group of African-American children playing along the sidewalk. As he approached, the children stopped playing and stood watching him. Besides looking different, he seemed different in other ways, not like an American, but like a foreigner of some kind. It was an almost totally black neighborhood. Joshua noticed the surprised look on their faces and smiled.

"Good day, little ones! You are such happy children. Always be happy. God made you to be happy. See all the beautiful things my Father has created just so you could enjoy them and be happy?"

"What beautiful things?" a skinny eight-year-old boy questioned cynically. "Everything around here is dirty and noisy. Even the buildings are falling apart."

"Yes, it is sad, isn't it," Joshua replied. "Someday you will live in a much nicer place, but even here there are beautiful things."

"Where?" the boy asked. "I don't see anything beautiful."

"What about Semantha?" who beamed when Joshua mentioned her name. "And Hakim? What about him? He's beautiful, too."

"She ain't beautiful. She's my sister. And Hakim? Hakim, yeah, man, you're beautiful. Wait till I tell everybody that this dude said you're beautiful."

"Quit it, Charles, or I'll tell everybody you still suck your thumb."

Joshua smiled. "You are all just having fun. Don't let your feelings get hurt when friends are playing with you. Just laugh."

"Mister, who are you, anyway?" Hakim asked. "We never saw you around here before. Besides, you're white. White people don't walk around here."

"I don't see color. I just see a beautiful creation of God. You are all beautiful. So, there are three things that are beautiful. Now look at that rosebush over there against the house. It's coming right out of the crack between the house and the concrete. Look at those roses, how red and brilliant they are. They even smell nice. Did you ever smell a rose?"

"No," Hakim replied.

After picking a rose off the bush, Joshua let them smell it.

"That smells nice," Hakim said with surprise.

Then the others smelled it. "Man, that smells pretty," Charles said.

Then Joshua gave the rose to Semantha. "Here, Semantha, God let that rosebush grow right out of the concrete just so He would have something beautiful to show you."

"What's your name? Who are you?" Charles asked.

"Joshua, that's my name. I have come to give people hope, to help them to be happy, because God wants His children to be happy."

"Mister, even if you're not a brother, you're nice. Will we see you again?" Hakim asked.

"I think so, someday," Joshua replied.

Finally, Semantha spoke up. "Joshua, how did you know our names when we didn't tell you?"

Joshua just smiled and answered softly, "I've known you for a long time."

As he began to walk away, he told them, "Be happy, always

be happy, and be kind . . . even to those who may seem different and unimportant!"

Joshua continued on his way. Stopping in front of a Baptist church not far up the street, he talked to a handful of people gathered around their minister, discussing possible renovations to the facade of their church.

"Hello," he said as he approached.

After turning to see who it was, one person returned the greeting. The others just continued their discussion. Joshua walked over to the man who greeted him.

"My name is Joshua. Thank you for being kind enough to say hello," he said as he extended a hand.

"I'm George, George Payne. I have to admit I was sort of surprised seeing someone who is not a brother walking down our neighborhood. Most people would be afraid."

"I am not afraid. I love all people. I see you are considering renovations to your church."

"Yes, they're badly needed. Have been for a long time, but only lately do we have a little bit of money saved to do the job. But now we don't know where to start."

"I am sure you will do a good job. I'll pray for it, George. And thank you for being so gracious toward a stranger."

"You're a nice man. May the Lord's peace be with you."

"Thank you, and with you as well."

As Joshua continued on his walk, he noticed the agents still following him, at a supposedly discreet distance. He merely smiled, knowing he already had them confused. The walk up North Capitol past the old waterworks led to an entirely different atmosphere, of colleges, churches, and monasteries, with even more monasteries and churches than around the immediate vicinity of the Vatican. It was also the site of a relatively new sanctuary dedicated to the Virgin Mary. As Joshua proceeded up the walkway toward the Romanesque marble structure, he knew this would completely baffle the agents following him. From a church where he talked to a Palestinian, to a Baptist church where he talked briefly to a black Baptist, and now to a Roman Catholic basilica. He knew what they were thinking: What do all these have in common? It doesn't make sense. What's his point? What is he doing now, at a Catholic place, after meeting an Arab man and stopping to talk at a black Baptist place?

Once inside the church, Joshua looked up at the huge, brilliant mosaic on the vaulted ceiling above the main altar. His peaceful look quickly changed to an uncomfortable grimace, showing his displeasure with the artist's idea of Jesus. Joshua knew that even at the Last Judgment, Jesus' love and compassion would still triumph even as people's consciences convicted them of self-centered sinfulness in the presence of Eternal Goodness.

As Joshua looked around at the magnificent structure, his face lighted up with a smile of pride at the honor paid his mother by the millions of tiny gifts from the simple poor who made all these tokens of love possible. He walked over to the reproduction of Michelangelo's *Pietà* and looked tenderly at the powerful portrayal of his mother's sorrow and grief as she held her son's dead body on her lap. Tears came to his eyes.

"Mother, not a day passes that I don't recall the pain and anguish my life caused you, especially during those last few hours. My heart forever aches when I think of it. At that moment, Mother, you held in your lap the sufferings of the whole world, as you became the mother of all those who were to become my brothers and sisters. People still need your tenderness, especially mothers and those who have no mothers. As you were always by my side, so now you must be part of what I am about to do. The world is in a sorry state, and the deep wounds need the healing warmth of a mother's love. There are many innocent people whose lives are being destroyed by those who consider themselves righteous and patriotic. Their families need your care, the way you cared for me when I was hurting."

People standing around were mesmerized by the intensity of Joshua's concentration. There was something inspiring yet humbling about him when he prayed. His face became trans-figured and radiant. Even the agents hiding behind nearby columns were impressed with what they saw, which confused them, causing them to wonder for a moment if he wasn't just a simple good man. But those who track evil in people do not easily give in to feelings of compassion.

"What is this guy?" Tom muttered to his partner. "Maybe he just has a thing with religion? He said he's a Jew, but here he is in a Catholic church, praying before a statue of Mary. Before he was talking to a Baptist. In the other church he met an Arab. What's up with this guy, anyway? He sure is strange. Do you think he could be casing the place, planning something?"

"That doesn't make sense," Dan remarked. "They don't blow up Catholic churches. The Vatican has always defended their people."

"But you're assuming he's a Palestinian. He said he's a Jew," Tom replied. "There's something about him that doesn't add up. It'll be interesting to see where he hangs out tonight."

After leaving the basilica, Joshua walked across town to Rock Creek Park. As he headed down into the park, the agents could not find a place to park. With darkness coming on, Joshua easily slipped from their sight. When they went looking for him early the next morning, he was nowhere to be found, which made them even more concerned. They asked people wandering in the park if they had seen a man fitting his description. Their question merely produced bewildered looks. He could not have just vanished. But where could he have gone? Driving around the streets looking for him proved a waste of time.

By early afternoon, Joshua was near a monastery in the northwest corner on Webster Street. In the field behind the monastery, young theology students were playing football. Joshua stood on the sideline and watched. Before long, someone asked if he would like to play, as they were a man short. Delighted, he ran out on the field as they all greeted him.

"What's your name?" a fellow asked him.

"Joshua."

"My name's Andre. I'm a priest, but they let me play since they needed a man. Would you like to play on the line?"

"Okay," Joshua answered.

In the huddle, they asked Joshua if he was a good catch.

"Try me; I think I might be able to. I've been good at catching things," he replied with a smile.

"No one will be expecting you, so I'll pass to you. Run as far as you can, then turn around," the captain told him.

After lining up, the quarterback called the numbers: "Twenty-one, sixty-eight, forty."

Joshua took off like a deer, running diagonally across the field. No one expected him to be a receiver, so there was no one anywhere near him. Like clockwork, the ball came flying toward him. As he reached out to catch it, the ball bounced off his hands up into the air. He ran in its direction, and as two others were closing in, he bounced off them, reached up and caught the ball, one yard from the goal, then walked across the goal line.

"Hey, you're good! You should come over every day,"

Andre said to him as he slapped him on the back. "I guess you play a lot?"

"First time," Joshua responded with a laugh. Of course, no one believed him. "It's fun," he continued.

Enjoying his friendly humor, they all laughed.

After the game, they invited Joshua into their community room for refreshments. As they sat around chatting, the young monks were curious about their friendly stranger.

"You live around here?" asked a tall, lanky fellow named Matt.

"Not really. I travel a lot."

"What brought you up here to our neck of the woods?"

"Your monks have always been devoted to my mother. I knew I would feel at home here, so I stopped by to visit."

No one picked up on the implication of what he was saying, and he continued, "Also, this is one of only a few seminaries that teach about Jesus. Others teach the theology about him, but not about the real, living Jesus whom the Jewish people experienced when he came walking down the street in their villages. Young priests have to experience the real Jesus, as Good Shepherd, if they are to avoid treating people the way the scribes and Pharisees treated the people of old."

"Yes, we have been blessed," said one of the young priests. "Years ago, one of our professors taught a class in which he shared with us his immense understanding of Jesus. He made Jesus real. It was almost like living with Jesus the way he spoke of him, as if he were his best friend or a next-door neighbor. It has had a lasting effect on our lives as religious, and especially as priests."

"You are also called the Brothers of Mary, Jesus' mother. I like that," Joshua said. "Many years ago I used to visit Mount Carmel, where Elijah gathered around him a group of young followers. Mary also visited there, occasionally with John, to whom Jesus entrusted his mother. Holy men lived in those caves from the time of Elijah, an inspiration to everyone who visited and prayed with them. It is still true even today. Now they are dedicated to following Mary's example by bringing Jesus alive again to a world that needs him more than ever. In fidelity to your own mission, imitate his mother and make him real for people."

Having accomplished his purpose in visiting the monks, Joshua took his leave and left the monastery. For the rest of the day, the friars spoke of nothing else but this strange man who could talk about scripture as if he had been there when it all happened. A short time later Joshua appeared across town, approaching a mosque. The security agents had given up trying to find him in the park. Not surprisingly they decided to hang around the same nearby mosque, suspecting that sooner or later he would show up there. Traveling back streets, he took a perfectly direct route to his destination, even though it took him two hours to reach the place. To the agents' delight, Joshua was heading straight for the mosque on Kenilworth Avenue. Unsuspectingly, however, the agents were falling right into a trap Joshua was laying for them.

After entering the mosque, which had been holding a special service that day, Joshua took off his sandals, went into the sanctuary, and said a silent prayer to his Father, the same God true Muslims worship. The Koran was composed of stories and teachings from the Hebrew Bible and the Gospels. But the God of Islam is the same as the Hebrew-Christian God. In the far corner of the sanctuary, a man was finishing his prayers. As he rose and turned, he saw Joshua, who walked toward him and introduced himself.

The man was gracious and responded in kind, telling Joshua

his name was Abboud, Rashid Abboud, and that his father had built this mosque many years ago when Rashid was only a child. Now he and all his family were still devoted members, although his wife and children were Christians.

"What can I do for you, Joshua?" Rashid asked.

"I would like to talk with you in private if I may."

"Of course. Could you tell me what the matter might be?" the man asked.

"Yes, I will share it with you briefly. I am Jewish. I am deeply concerned about the terrible tragedy that has befallen all our people, and I would like to share with you some thoughts that I think could be of great importance."

"Well, I am on my way home. If you like, you can accompany me, and we can talk along the way."

"That would be fine. I am grateful to you for your kindness, and to a stranger whom you have never met," Joshua replied.

Rashid's family was second-generation Syrian, respectable people who had worked hard to establish themselves in their new country. Industrious and frugal, they had saved enough to send their children to good schools. Their oldest boy, Ammed, was a computer engineer working for the government. The two older girls, Fatima and Miriam, were still in college, both honor students. Two other children, Sharon and Vera, were seven and five, respectively. They were still at home.

As the car parked, two children came running out of the house.

"Uncle Rashi, Uncle Rashi, we were waiting for you," they shouted as they ran into his arms.

"I met this nice man and we talked for a while. That's why I'm late," Rashid told them as he lifted them up, kissed them, and carried them toward the house.

"Come with us, Joshua!" he said as he turned and saw Joshua still standing near the car.

"I am so surprised to see you," Rashid said to the children. "I didn't know you were coming over today. Are your parents with you? I hope you are staying for dinner?"

"Oh yes, Aunt Miriam wanted to surprise you and asked if we could spend the day with you. We all went to Mass together while you were at your services, and she insisted we come home with her."

The children were the two daughters of Sophie, Rashid's younger sister, who was married to Miriam's brother, Rafael Chamoun. They were, like so many Middle Eastern families, one extended family and very close to one another.

"Welcome home, dear," Miriam said as she kissed her husband. She stepped back so Rafael and Sophie could give him their double-cheek kisses.

"How nice! With all the bad news about our families back home, you are the best medicine in the world. I am so glad you came over. I would like to introduce a new friend I met at services today. His name is Joshua, and he is Jewish."

It was as if they had all been hit on the head with a brick. A Jew at our family's Sunday meal, they all thought. How could he invite a Jew into our house, and at our Sunday family dinner?

"I know what you are all thinking. Please don't be upset. I haven't lost my mind. I am sure once you get to know him you will understand. I know I should not have just dropped this surprise on you so abruptly, but circumstances just happened and I made the decision I knew I should make. Please trust me and welcome our guest. It is part of our culture, remember." As Rashid introduced his family to Joshua, the atmosphere slowly warmed.

Joshua knew it would be a tense situation, but he had no time to waste being overly delicate. There was too much to be done, too many important things to be accomplished, and in so short a time.

Rashid asked his family to excuse him and Joshua, as he would like to spend time with his guest alone because they had many things to talk about. The two went into Rashid's study, where a beautiful Persian rug struck Joshua's eyes as he entered.

"What a magnificent work of art!" he said, captivated by the striking combination of designs and colors.

"Yes, it was handmade by my great-grandmother and her sisters many years ago. It took them five years, working every day, to finish the job. It is a masterpiece."

Rashid gestured for Joshua to sit in the soft leather chair next to the fireplace, while he sat in a rocking chair facing his guest.

"All right, Joshua, now that we have peace and quiet, what are these world-shaking ideas you wanted to share with me?"

"Rashid, I know you have vast influence in the Arabic community all across the country. You are a wise man and have a reputation for kindness, generosity, and great integrity. What I propose to you is very simple, though not easy."

"What is that?" Rashid asked.

"To meet with Jewish leaders in our communities, not just locally, but throughout the country, and talk to them about peace. The second part of the plan is to start a movement of American Jews and Arabs to work for peace. If something is not done, Arabs and Jews will just keep killing one another. It will never end. Revenge knows neither Sabbath rest nor sacred days."

"Who would ever think of such a thing, Jews and Arabs in America meeting to work for peace," Rashid responded. "It *is* a remarkable idea. It just might work. I know that Jewish people are just as concerned as we are that it come to an end, with justice for everyone. Politicians can't do it. They are interested only in who can deliver for them the most votes. How would we go about such a thing, Joshua?"

"We would have to find interested Jewish people. There are many who would be only too happy to work on a project like this. One of the first things the group would have to do is pressure the president to work for a just solution, and not a forced political compromise favoring only one side. Leave it up to me to find Jewish people who would be interested."

"Joshua, I think it just might work."

"My friend, I must leave now. There is much to be done. I will see you soon."

The two men hugged and parted. As Joshua was leaving, Rashid asked if he could drive him somewhere. Joshua declined, saying he had transportation.

As he walked down the street, he noticed his shadows not far behind on the opposite side of the street. They let him reach the corner, then started their car to follow him. By the time they reached the corner, Joshua had already turned and was nowhere in sight.

"Where did he go this time?" Dan said with anger and frustration. "There's no place for him to hide. He just this minute turned the corner. He couldn't have gone into a building. There is no alley for him to run into. Again he just evaporated into thin air. This guy has to be up to something, and there's no way we can pin him down."

"We just have to be faster," Tom responded, trying to calm his partner. "He must know we're following him, and all he needs is one unguarded moment to give us the slip. This guy's a fox."

T HE SEARCH FOR JOSHUA WAS FUTILE. THE TWO MEN called their superior for instructions and were told to covertly pin a transmitter on him when they found him. Finding him was the problem. He could be anywhere. It was days before another agent phoned Dan Halloran and told him he thought he had spotted their man. It was in another section of the city, and he was coming out of a synagogue. Dan asked his friend if he still had him in sight. No, but he should not be far from the synagogue, as he was walking leisurely down the street. Would they keep an eye on him until they got there? He promised to do his best, and they hung up.

"Now, what is he doing in a synagogue?" Dan asked his partner.

"Don't ask me! I'm just as bewildered as you are. We're going to look like a couple of incompetents back at the office if we keep losing him. This fellow makes me feel like an amateur.

And he isn't even driving a car. He's only walking the street and we still can't keep track of him."

The agents crossed over to Arlington, where their colleague had directed them. As they drove down the street, they spotted Joshua and immediately called the other agent.

"That's the man," Dan said with a deep sense of relief. "I owe you one, Charlie. I think this character is up to something interesting. He's as slippery as an eel. I hope we can keep an eye on him. The boss told us to find some excuse to accost him and secretly pin a transmitter and a bug on him. Well, thanks. We owe you a good one for this."

"Don't worry! I'll remind you. Take care, you guys. Mickey and I have to get back to the office. We're already late."

As before, Joshua knew immediately that he was being followed, but it bothered him not in the slightest. In fact, though he was contacting the people he wanted to, he was also playing a game with the agents, a game that would end in a fascinating predicament.

This particular day was the next Sabbath. People were beginning to gather in front of the synagogue. It was a warm day, and a perfect morning to stand outside the synagogue before the service and chat with friends while waiting for the rabbi to come. Joshua walked over and introduced himself, using only his first name, of course. The others welcomed him, asking him a host of questions, not to be rude, but as a way of welcoming him by showing their interest. Joshua was more open in sharing with them than he was with the agents, who, from their surveillance equipment in their car not far removed, could hear the conversations. Joshua knew they could not make out a thing that was being said because too many people were talking at the same time, and his voice was lost in the babble, which annoyed the agents considerably. At one point, he was speaking in Hebrew to a man who had just arrived from Israel. This also the agents could not detect too clearly, though they assumed it was Hebrew.

Before long the rabbi, a woman in her late thirties, walked over to the small group and was introduced to Joshua, as a guest from Bethlehem. She warmly welcomed him to the synagogue and invited him, if he was so inclined, to join their congregation. Joshua thanked the rabbi and the others for being so gracious and said he would enjoy attending whenever he was in the neighborhood. With that, people began filing into the building, and in a few minutes the service began, promptly on time, as the rabbi was always most punctual.

"I am sure almost all of you here today know me, but in case we have visitors or guests for the first time, my name is Rabbi Rapkin. I know most of the congregation calls me 'Rabbi,' but I do have a first name, which I would happily respond to. My name is Marsha. With that I would like to begin the service."

The rabbi was an alert and friendly individual, so when two men dressed in dark suits appeared at the entrance to the sanctuary, she noticed them immediately and welcomed them most cordially, inviting them to sit wherever they might like. The two men were completely befuddled, especially as half the synagogue turned to see who they were. They wanted to turn and crawl out, but it was too late. They had already lost their cover, so they made as if they were coming to worship. One of the ushers escorted them up the aisle to two empty seats, which happened to be right next to Joshua.

"Welcome, gentlemen!" Joshua said to them with a devilish grin. "I didn't realize that you were both Jewish. I would have taken you for Irish or English. But then perhaps you are converts to Judaism. Whatever, it is good that you take your religion so seriously. It is also nice that we can worship God together."

If stares were stilettos, the agents' looks would have stabbed him through and through. As the service progressed, however, the agents were again impressed with Joshua's piety. They were also impressed to hear him respond with what seemed to be perfect responses to some of the prayers in what they were now sure was Hebrew.

At one point in the service, the rabbi welcomed all the visitors and asked their names and where they were from. When she asked Joshua, he simply said, "My name is Joshua ben-Youssef. I was born in Bethlehem and have spent a good part of my life in this beautiful country."

When she asked the two agents, they were at a complete loss. They could ill afford to be honest. All they managed to say was, "We both live in the city, and thought we would stop in and pray with you."

"We are a very open community here," the rabbi replied, "and you seem like such good young men. How wonderful that you pray and worship together. In our synagogue we pray for such relationships. In our community prayers this morning, we will all pray that Yahweh will bless your very special friendship."

The men were discomfited at the inference, while Joshua had all he could do to keep from laughing at the awkward situation.

The service was pleasant enough, as are most synagogue services. Rabbi Rapkin delivered an eloquent sermon on the need for justice and forgiveness in a world that has forgotten the meaning of those splendid virtues that most reflect the divine in a human being, virtues that have sadly been replaced by retribution and self-righteous arrogance. She was clearly referring to the prevailing political attitudes, which she felt were a betrayal of the gentle, forgiving Jesus whom Christians were sworn to imitate.

"They are virtues," she said, "which we as Jews could well imitate from the life of the Jewish man Jesus, a man who I am proud to boast is one of our own. It is his message of forgiveness that our world needs to heed, because most of the problems in the world today are caused by political leaders' refusal to heal injustice and to extend the hand of forgiveness to enemies. Someday someone in a position of authority will take Jesus' message seriously enough to try it. Then the world will be surprised by how true his words are. The problem with Jesus' message is that few people, even among his followers, have ever tried it."

The agents were surprised at the words of the rabbi, but though both were Christians they were not offended. In fact, they were impressed with the rabbi's insight into the essence of Jesus' message, a message that is ridiculed by cynics as unreasonable and unrealistic.

After the service, the congregation filed out to the hall for refreshments. The agents left immediately, but only to wait outside in an inconspicuous spot until Joshua came out, which was not for a while, as he had people to meet inside.

It was remarkable how comfortably Joshua could mingle with people who were strangers just a few minutes before. While walking among the group, he felt very much at home. The folks at this synagogue were very open to the world and had lost the narrow tribal mentality that can so often imprison minds and hearts behind barriers of family and tribal prejudices. Being so open, they were interested not just in their own people, but in the injustice being done to others and were not afraid to speak about it. These were the kind of people Joshua needed to talk to. He went from one small group to another during the social gathering. As he listened and shared, the people's curiosity was aroused. A large group gathered around him to hear what he had to say. He was clearly a man with a purpose. What was his intention in coming to their synagogue?

"We like the way you talk, sir. What did you say your name is? Do you live nearby?" an elderly man asked him.

"My name is Joshua. I have long known of your people here, and I wanted very much to visit with you. That is why I came here today. I know you are all curious as to why I came. It is very simple. I have many things to share with you. One is the plight of our people, and the plight of all the people in the Middle East. It seems no one knows where to begin to stop the terrible scandal of the children of Abraham destroying one another. And so many wonderful things could happen if they would only work together. They are both rich in resources, different resources, which complement one another. They both need what the other has. We could all use our influence to bring about a climate of change. That is my dream."

This was what the agents following Joshua should have heard, but they were not there. Joshua freely expressed his concerns about the troubles springing up around the world like a virus. The fabric of civility that had been carefully built up among nations over decades of careful, sensitive diplomacy was rapidly unraveling in the face of boorish insults and reckless decisions that ignored prudent and carefully thought-out advice.

The elderly man spoke up and commented about Joshua's remarks. "You have said things, sir, that have been on my mind for a long time. I was afraid to express them, but you expounded on them so eloquently. We would hear more of what you have to say."

"Mr. Greenberg, I am impressed with the honesty of your mind," Joshua was saying as two synagogue officials were approaching the group surrounding him. "You have a rare ability to see truth and embrace it. So many others are frightened by truth because it may force them to think differently and perhaps change their beliefs or way of living. You are one who not only is not afraid of truth, but reaches out to embrace it, regardless of where it leads. People can trust one like you."

"Thank you, Joshua," replied the elderly gentleman. "I have always tried to be honest with myself, 'true to myself,' as some people like to say. It is always better that way. Yes, I am concerned about the state of affairs today, and I would love to be in a position where I could do something about it. But I would not know where to start."

"We start by discussing with friends our concerns," Joshua replied. "Each of us is important. Our concern is important. It is surprising how many people can identify with a concern carefully expressed about a current issue of vital importance. Most people have an innate sense of justice, but few have the ability to analyze a situation and see the injustice. When someone points it out, however, it becomes very clear to many other people. And when people gather together to demand change, things do change."

"You are right there, young man. I have seen that many times."

One of the synagogue leaders standing by and listening made the suggestion to gather on one of the nights in the coming week to discuss current issues. Everyone thought it was a good idea, so Wednesday night was decided upon for their first meeting. Almost a dozen people said they would come.

Joshua was pleased at the success of his first encounter with the Jewish community and looked forward with enthusiasm to their meeting.

4

LEAVING THE SYNAGOGUE, JOSHUA SPOTTED THE AGENTS' car not far down the street. He walked in the opposite direction at a fast pace and turned the corner. Just past the second house, an alley led to the back of the synagogue that exited out on the next street. In no time, he was out of sight. Again the agents lost his trail. Annoyed, they determined this would be the last time they would let him just disappear right from under their noses. Frustrated, they wandered the neighborhood for the better part of an hour, asking people walking along if they had seen anyone fitting his description. But no one had seen him. Again they contacted their colleagues, but they were too busy with their own surveillance and could not leave their location to help.

"We might as well go back to the office," Dan said, discouraged and still irritated at the embarrassing incident in the synagogue. Tom said nothing, just grunted his okay. He was too dejected even to speak. It was a quiet ride back to headquarters, where they knew they would take more heat from their fellow agents.

"Shall we stop and get lunch? We haven't had anything all day," Dan said to his partner.

"Might as well. We're not going to accomplish anything else today. No use going back early. What'll we do there?" Tom replied.

"We could look through the files and the computer for any information on this guy. Who knows, there may be something, and we might just get lucky," Dan suggested.

"Sounds like a good idea."

The men stopped off for lunch, then returned to the office to search the computer for any relevant data about a Joshua ben-Youssef. It was almost as difficult finding anything about him on the computer as it was trying to track him down on the city streets. Amazingly, not even their vast database had anything on this man. Apparently he was an unknown entity in any important spheres on the American scene. It was almost as if he weren't even real. Finally, after three hours they found something about a strange man who had been in San Francisco in the recent past. He kept telling people about an impending earthquake, which actually took place just as he had predicted. Comments from various clergy described him as an oddball not to be taken seriously. Only one old priest had anything good to say about him, but that priest was out of favor with diocesan officials. Only the homeless had any respect for him, and that was probably because he seemed like one of them. Other than that, there was nothing to be found in the computer.

Later that day, the two agents wandered the neighborhoods where Joshua had made his latest contacts. He undoubtedly would be in either of those two places. So they drove out and scoured the locations. Late in the afternoon, just before their duty was over, they spotted him.

"What is it with this guy? It's almost as if he's playing a game with us. We've been looking high and low for him all day, then he just appears as if he knows it's quitting time. What'll we do now, follow him or call it a day?"

"We don't have much choice. I want to wrap this thing up. We might as well follow him for a while, see where he goes. Maybe we'll have some luck."

They followed Joshua at a discreet distance, watching his every move. Suddenly, a black limousine stopped just ahead of Joshua and turned toward the curb. It was obviously by arrangement. Unsurprised, Joshua walked over and got in. The car took off immediately.

"Well, finally we're getting some action," Dan Halloran said excitedly. "We're finally hitting pay dirt."

"Don't be too sure," Tom cautioned. "I wouldn't be too quick to jump to conclusions. He only got into a car. Could be a friend. As suspicious as everything looks, remember, he hasn't done anything wrong yet. Could be totally innocent at the end of all our trouble."

"How could he be innocent? Look at all the people he's been contacting. They all have to do with the Middle East in some way: the Arab in the church; the visit to the mosque, as if he already had contacts there; the visit to the synagogue, where he gets heavily involved in conversation with people he must have already known. You just don't go visiting in a strange city and start making contacts unless you know what you're doing and where you're going and who you're scheduled to meet. This fellow's obviously been planning this whole thing for a long time. How would he have all these contacts if he didn't know of them and their whereabouts beforehand? I know we're on to something."

"I wouldn't be too sure, Dan. There are a lot of things that just don't mesh. Like why is he visiting Jews, and why does he go to a synagogue to pray? Another thing we haven't found out yet is where he stays at night. He always disappears when it gets dark. Maybe we'll find out this time if we don't lose that limo."

Tom Clark called headquarters and gave them the license plate number of the limousine. In no time he had the name of the owner, a certain Ibrahim Abdul. Who was Ibrahim Abdul? The computer check revealed that he was a wealthy import-export executive who had myriad contacts not only in the Middle East, but in various countries in Africa and France and Eastern Europe. He was not a Muslim, but a Lebanese Catholic.

"See, it's already getting complicated," Dan said. "What would a wealthy Arab with all kinds of suspicious contacts want with an apparently homeless man unless they're planning for him to carry out some kind of covert operation? This guy is clearly a terrorist of some kind."

"Dan, cool it! You sound like Senator Joe McCarthy back in the late fifties. That's the way he used to talk. After starting out trying to do good in ferreting out real Communists, he ended up destroying a lot of innocent people as well."

"Well, to me it makes a lot of sense. Maybe you can't see it, but to me it's obvious they're planning something. We just have to find out what it is."

"They're turning the corner. Don't lose them," Tom said excitedly.

Dan turned the corner and still had the car in view. They followed it all the way to Silver Spring, where they ended up at a mansion just outside the city. According to the computer report, it was the home of Ibrahim Abdul.

"Well, this is nice," Tom said, disgusted. "All the way up here and it looks like we finally got something, and we're stuck here in the street while they're in there doing whatever they're doing, and we don't have a clue. We can't go in there. We're already overtime, and I'm starved. What do we do now? Stay here till he leaves? Go back, check in, call it a day, and lose him? Or call the boss and ask for instructions?"

"We could ask him to send replacements so we can go home and get some sleep," Dan thought out loud. "But then we'd still have to wait here until they found somebody to send out. Why don't we just call in, tell them what happened, and if they send somebody, we can call it a day and get home." Which was what they did.

After an hour or so, their replacements arrived. Tom brought them up-to-date, and he and Dan left for the night. Joshua stayed at the mansion all through the night. Early the next morning, the limousine left the estate and drove down to the local Catholic church, where the whole family emerged from the car and entered the church in time for early mass. But Joshua was not with them, and no one else was in the car.

A short time later, Dan and Tom arrived at the Abdul estate. Their overnight replacements were not in a happy mood. The boss had sent Tom's friend Mickey Schurman and his partner, Charlie Haggerty, to cover the mansion through the night.

The men emerged from their cars.

Tom said to his friend, "Thanks again for covering for us. We needed a good night's sleep."

"Judging from our few hours on the job, we could tell this is not a happy assignment," Mickey said.

"What happened? You guys look miserable," Tom commented.

"We sat here the whole darn night. What a waste of time!"

Mickey complained. When he told them about following the limo to the church, and the whole family getting out except Joshua, Tom and Dan had to laugh. As annoying as it was, it was funny. They knew Joshua had to have slipped out right after the family left the house.

"No use wasting time here," Tom said. "We might as well start all over again. This is the most exasperating assignment I ever had. How in heaven can we track this guy? It's like trying to catch a fish with your bare hands. It's as if he knows every move we make or are going to make."

"If he left the house within the past couple of hours, he can't be too far, since he walks wherever he has to go. We'll just drive around the neighborhood," Dan said. "If we're lucky, we'll catch up with him."

"Good idea! Let's give it a try."

After saying good-bye to their friends, they got back into their car and started down the street. They had to scour the neighborhood for well over an hour, but finally they spotted him walking in the direction of Rock Creek Park. They parked their car and followed on foot, eventually ending up in the park, where Joshua wandered around watching the birds and chipmunks for the better part of the next two hours. It was almost three o'clock. Finally, he sat on a bench near a picnic area and ate his lunch while watching a family celebrating a birthday party.

"That does it," Dan complained. "That fellow brings his lunch with him and we're starving. Do we have anything in the car?"

"Luckily, I brought a couple of sandwiches my wife made. If we're going to be following him on foot, we better eat something."

Tom went to get the sandwiches and returned fifteen minutes later. "I have two different kinds of sandwiches," he said, "ham and cheese and a roast beef."

"Why don't we split them, so we can have some of each?"

"Good. I also have a thermos of coffee."

"Not bad. We can at least have a picnic," Dan concluded with a smile.

While Tom was away, Dan had watched Joshua like a hawk. No way would he let him slip through his fingers again. But shortly after Tom left, an odd thing happened. Joshua left the picnic bench and walked over to a small stand of birch trees, where he sat down and started talking out loud. He spoke quietly, but it was loud enough for Dan to hear every word.

"Mother, I think this is a time when you can help me. Those people in the detention center I am concerned about are innocent. Their families are suffering cruelly as they see their loved ones imprisoned unjustly. While I'm doing what I have to do, I would like you to visit them and bring them comfort. They will at first be shocked, but they will listen. Some of them are Christians, but most are Muslims. But they are good people. They are taught in their Koran to respect you. It is part of their religion, so they will be pleased that you show concern for them. Some have been detained locally. They are frightened and under terrible stress. Some have relatives in the local mosque where I have friends. If you could visit them, I would be happy, and when word gets back to their families it will bring them great comfort. . . . Yes, Mother, that is the place. Go to them! There are some there who are evil, but they will not see you, only the innocent ones will."

The agent, seeing no one, only Joshua talking to himself, concluded that he was a disturbed person, which made him potentially even more dangerous than he and his partner had originally thought. Tom was coming down the path as Joshua finished speaking. As they ate their lunch, Dan briefed him on what he had just witnessed.

"You just missed it, Tom. This guy was talking to some invisible person. I think he's mental, which frightens me even more."

"What was he talking about? Who was he talking to?" Tom asked.

"I don't know. It seemed like he was talking to someone mentioned in the Koran, but I'm not sure. He was talking about the person going to visit Muslim detainees, and especially to detainees in a local detention center. That clinches it for me. He's no Jew. He has to be a Muslim. I am convinced more than ever there is something going on. We've got to get to the bottom of it."

Tom was more interested in his food than in what his partner had to say. Dan had the habit of seeing plots and conspiracies too easily, and Tom ended up having to check his facts to make sure they were accurate and not invented to prove a supposed plot. He was always hoping that Dan would outgrow the need to see a conspiracy behind every person they were investigating, because his partner was otherwise a good man, with proper morals and a sense of decency.

"Come on, Dan, eat your lunch. We'll watch him more closely and see if pieces we put together make any sense."

Joshua wandered through the park for the rest of the day, chatting with people he met along the pathways. At one point he stopped off at a picnic area and said hello to a group of young people having a good time with their friends and praised them for their wholesome sense of fun. Among the group was a pretty young lady with reddish hair and a happy, childlike spirit. She seemed to be the spark that ignited the whole group with their joyful spirit. Joshua called her by name, which shocked her.

"How do you know my name?"

Joshua laughed. "I knew you before you were born. One day you will do my work. Your spirit is what the world needs. You are a gift of God to heal and comfort many hearts."

While the group was talking about what Joshua had just said, he slipped quietly away and wandered along the path.

As the evening approached and darkness began to set in, he returned to the sheltered grove of birch trees where he had rested earlier. He opened a backpack he had been carrying, took out a microweave blanket, spread it on the ground, and sat down to rest. Looking out across the park, he began to speak out loud.

"Sounds like he's praying," Tom said.

"I thought Muslims knelt on a prayer rug," Dan commented.

Dan wondered if he was truly praying or just doing some kind of Eastern-type exercise. Dan's mind was already made up that he was a terrorist. When you like someone, that person can do no wrong. When you do not like someone, everything the person does is either strange or suspect.

Joshua gave not the slightest hint that he knew the agents were nearby. After his apparent soliloquy, he took a small loaf of bread and a bottle of wine out of his knapsack and began eating, much to the annoyance of the agents, who expected him to just rest there and then go someplace to spend the night. It was looking very much as if he were going to spend the night in the park, which was exactly what he did.

"I've had it," Dan said in utter disgust. "I have never had an assignment like this. I just feel in my bones this guy knows we're tailing him and he's determined to make it as miserable as possible for us."

"Dan, cool it! You're really getting paranoid now. How could he possibly know we're following him?"

"Well, look at him! Most people, even terrorists, would spend the night in a hotel or at a friend's house, but not this guy. He's got to spend it in the woods. So we're stuck in the woods all night, in our suits. It is so ridiculous. We can't even get replacements out here without alerting him that he's being followed. We have to just sit here all night like stooges and watch him enjoying his sleep. We can't even sneeze or cough or, God forbid, snore. Which means we have to stay awake all night, while this guy gets a good night's sleep."

Tom could not help but laugh quietly at his friend's logic, which made a certain sense if his premise was true, that their suspect knew they were following him. But since that was not obvious to Tom, he had to laugh at Dan's frustration at the thought of not being able to get a night's rest.

All during the night, the two men made sure neither of them slept soundly, for fear of snoring. At the slightest hint of a snore, the one awake would wake his partner. As the sun came up and light suffused the trees, Joshua was nowhere to be found. The resulting frustration could be heard all through the park, in language not fit for pious ears. Joshua emerged from the park with a broad grin and continued walking up the street. By the time the agents returned to their car and drove away, Joshua had already turned down a side street.

5

I T WAS DURING A SHORT PERIOD OF RECREATION AT A DE-
tention camp in northern Virginia that a strange phenomenon occurred. Committed Muslim activists automatically found
one another and stayed by themselves during the exercise time.
The other people arrested at random from their homes or
places of work seemed confused and lost. They, too, found one
another and stayed together in another corner of the large
room, which at one time may have been a gym. Over two
dozen of them were talking casually, decrying the injustice they
felt over being kidnapped so arbitrarily by federal officials. They
had been law-abiding citizens all their lives and had worked
hard and enjoyed their freedom in what was for them a paradise compared with what some of them and their families had
experienced back in their Middle East homeland. Now it was
all destroyed. Their reputations were ruined, their wives and
children disillusioned and frightened about their future. As the
men talked, a figure walked quietly toward the group and un-

obtrusively sat in an empty seat in the circle. It was a woman, a woman with a look of innocent beauty and compassion. She was clothed in Middle Eastern dress. She had black hair, deep hazel eyes, and a complexion like alabaster, almost translucent.

The men were startled but prudently showed no outward sign that anything unusual was taking place.

"Salaam, peace," the woman said. The voice was calm, reassuring.

The men were surprised that no one else in the room had noticed the woman's presence. Looking at one another to see if they all saw the woman, they said nothing; but as everyone was looking in her direction, they knew it was an experience they all shared.

"Who are you?" asked an elderly man.

"My name is Miriam. You know me. Those of you who are Christian know my son well. You who are Muslim know me from your Koran. I come to tell you that my son asked me to visit with you and assure you that nothing evil will happen to you. As your captors realize they have done you an injustice, out of shame they will release you and you will be free. Do not worry about your reputations. My son will make sure they are restored. In the meantime, take heart and do not be afraid. Your families will also know what I have just told you. When you leave, it is important that you dedicate your lives to justice and mercy and the forgiveness my son has always preached. It is his message of forgiveness and justice that will make peace possible throughout the world. War solves no problems. It only extends and intensifies the hatred. Strive and pray for peace, peace based on justice."

The woman then left just as suddenly as she had appeared. The men became like a disturbed beehive, the Muslim men excitedly asking the men who were Lebanese Maronite Christians who was the lady's son she had mentioned.

"It could only be Mary, Miriam, Jesus' mother," responded a middle-aged man named Naim.

"You mean the Virgin Mother of Jesus, the one Muhammad talked about in our sacred book?" a young Muslim asked.

"Yes, it has to be her. What other woman would slip in here unnoticed and talk to us?"

"I know it had to be her," Naim insisted. "A friend, a Polish Carmelite priest who had been in Dachau, that terrible concentration camp, twice experienced her presence when he collapsed in the field while returning one night with the prisoners from a work detail. In the middle of the night, as he lay in the field, Jesus' mother appeared to him and told him to quickly return to his barracks and not to worry, that the prisoners would be saved. That happened to him two times. The second time it happened was the night before the Americans came to liberate them. He had again collapsed and fallen in the mud when returning from work with the others. The Americans were expected to reach the camp by nine o'clock. The commandant had been planning to have everyone executed before the Americans arrived, so there would be no witnesses. Again in the middle of the night, Miriam appeared to the priest as he lay in the mud. 'Marianus, Marianus'—that was his name; Marianus Nowakowski—'wake up, and go back to your barracks before they miss you. Tell the others not to worry. You will all be saved.' Then she disappeared."

"What happened?" asked the old man.

"The Americans came over an hour earlier than they were expected, and the whole camp, with the many thousands of prisoners, was liberated. Father Nowakowski was made the temporary mayor of all the liberated prisoners, and it was his job to locate and reunite all of them with their families. And that is a true story. It seems Jesus' mother does deeds of compassion like that in times of great stress."

The men slept well that night after praying that the lady would visit their families and share with them the good news.

In the meantime, Joshua was on his way to his new Arab friend Rashid Abboud, who since their last meeting had been contacting influential friends who were active in various Arab communities, not only locally, but in other areas.

By now, the federal agents were beginning to sense a pattern in Joshua's wandering. The last time he was in the park area, he visited with the Arab family, so they roamed the vicinity hoping to find him. Their persistence paid off, as they found him walking toward Rashid Abboud's house.

"Joshua, my friend, I was hoping you might stop by today. I have some good news," Rashid said as he greeted him at the front door, kissing him on both cheeks.

"Greetings, my dear friend. I have some good news as well."

"Come inside and say hello to the family. They've been asking about you all week, especially the children. The family's all together again, like every Sunday."

This time the children were being coy, hiding behind a column at the entrance to the living room.

"Children, don't be so shy. You have been asking about Joshua all week long, and now that he's here, you've lost your tongues. Come over and see Joshua."

The two girls walked over and shyly lifted up their heads. Joshua stooped down to their level. Holding the younger girl by the shoulders, he looked at her and called her by name. "Vera, I've thought about you this week, and asked my Father to bless you and protect you."

Then he turned to her sister and held her by the shoulders. As she looked into his eyes, he said to her, "And you, Sharon, I know about the nice things you did the other day for those poor children at school."

The girl was shocked. "How do you know about those children?" she asked him.

"That's a secret, but it was a wonderful kindness you did. You gave the boy your favorite pen, because all the other children have nice things, and you wanted him to have something nice, too. And you gave your beautiful silk scarf to his sister so she would have something nice to hide the worn collar on her blouse. What was more important is that you did this in such a way that no one else noticed, and you made believe they were doing you a favor by accepting them. That is the kind of love my Father blesses. May you always be that way!"

"Thank you, Joshua."

"Joshua, I do nice things, too," Vera added hurriedly, hoping that Joshua would say something nice to her, too.

"I know you do, Vera. You are always nice to people. Every time someone comes to your house, you always give them something as they are leaving, either a peach, or an orange, or a little bag of pistachios. You are a very kind little girl."

"But I'm not little anymore. I am almost five years old, you know, this many," she said as she held up five fingers.

Joshua smiled.

"Well, children, you run along now," Rashid said. "Joshua and I have some very important business to discuss, and we do not want to be disturbed."

As the children skipped out toward the playroom, Rashid led Joshua into the kitchen to say hello to the women, who were busily discussing ingredients for the meal they were preparing together.

"Joshua," Miriam exclaimed excitedly, "how nice to see you again! My husband said you might be coming. Last week when you were here we had such a wonderful time. Our guests are here again, hoping you'd stop by."

"Yes, the girls talked about you all week and hoped they would see you again," Sophie added. "You made a big impression on us all."

"I was a stranger and you welcomed me," Joshua responded. "Even though you did not know me, you treated me as a friend."

"But that is what our religion teaches us," Miriam said. "Our families are old families from back home in the Middle East. Our ancestors knew Jesus and have passed on to us Jesus' original teaching on love and caring and forgiveness, so what we did was not new to us. It is the way we have been brought up since we were children."

"Your parents taught you well. All Jesus' followers should take his message to their hearts the way your families did. It would be a much better world to live in."

"Thank you, Joshua," said Sophie. "Even our relatives who are Muslim have found much beauty and goodness in what we teach our children, and they have often commented on how they can see it reflected in our children's behavior."

"I know you and Rashid have much to discuss," Miriam said. "Why don't you take care of your business now while we prepare dinner, so you can spend time with the whole family afterward? We would all like to enjoy visiting with our guest."

"Well, Joshua, we have been given our instructions," Rashid said, "so let us retire to our quiet little den and let the head of the house do her cooking."

"Rashid, you are such a subtle chauvinist," his wife said, half jesting.

On the way into the den, Rashid stole a plate of hors d'oeuvres from the counter and walked off with Joshua.

"Well, Joshua, what kind of week did you have?"

"I had quite an adventure. Between visiting different people and attending services at a synagogue, and evading government agents, I had a most enjoyable week."

"I spent a very busy week doing my homework for our meeting today. I made some excellent contacts, people who are very interested in working with us. I think you met one of them already, Ibrahim?"

"Yes, he impressed me deeply, a very sincere man. He is excited about using his resources and contacts to help us. I will meet with him again soon. I also met with people at the synagogue over in Arlington. They too are willing to meet with us and see if they can help. All in all, I think we are off to a good start after only one week."

"Where do you think we should go from here?" Rashid asked him.

"First of all, we should bring together the people we have contacted so far for an initial meeting so we can all get acquainted and begin to feel comfortable together. We are still strangers to one another. It is important we learn more about one another and what we are attempting to accomplish. Do you have any suggestions about where we should have that first meeting?"

"Probably the best place to have it is at Ibrahim's house. He has plenty of room there and it is out of sight. If we gather a group of Middle Eastern–looking people in a crowded residential neighborhood, we are going to be immediately suspect, especially in the present political atmosphere. We have to be so careful today."

"Ibrahim's place is a good suggestion. Would you contact

him and make arrangements? I will give you the names and addresses of the people I have met so you can call them and give them the information. That should be a very profitable meeting."

"Joshua, last week when I met you and you shared your ideas with me, I have to admit, after thinking it over, that I thought you were a dreamer and that your ideas would never work. But I have changed my thinking on the matter. I know the ideas sound impractical and unrealistic, but I now have a very good feeling about them. I really think this can work."

"I know it will work, my friend. Thinking positively about it will inspire ways to make sure it works."

"What will be the last stage of the plan? Have you gotten that far yet?"

"I have my ideas, Rashid, but I would like you and your friends and the people I find to share their ideas and draw on their friends in high places to pave the way and offer practical assistance. The final phase of the plan and the strategy will be the sum of all your ideas and suggestions. In this way, everyone will have an important part to play."

"That is brilliant, Joshua," Rashid responded, "really brilliant. In that way, everyone will feel a sense of importance and that they are a necessary part of what is taking place. That would be a great way to run a corporation, everyone feeling needed for the success of the business. Where did you ever come up with such an idea?"

"I have always worked that way. I never treat people as pawns in a chess game. I form partnerships with people and hope they will accept me as their partner. Most people do not and insist on going it alone. It is unfortunate, because their life could be a most enjoyable adventure if they would only trust."

"You're a strange man, Joshua," said Rashid, "but a good man, a man with a kind heart. How many people would think of doing what you're doing? You have goodness in you that transcends other people's prejudices and hatreds."

"My friend, that is the only way this world will have peace, if people can learn to understand and forgive one another and not make nationality and race and political affiliation their religion."

"You are right," Rashid agreed. "I have seen families that were once close destroyed by fierce disagreements over those kinds of issues. And you still think we can be successful in trying to resolve one of the most vicious conflicts that has been waged between Arabs and Jews for centuries?"

"It will be a good start. Hatred is hard to uproot, especially when so many family members have been brutally murdered on both sides. But a beginning has to be made, and goodwill and concern for the children and the grandchildren will carry the movement forward, hopefully."

"We have to hope for that. When people want peace badly enough, peace will happen. It has to come from hearts with goodwill."

The rest of the afternoon with Rashid's family went well. Joshua enjoyed himself immensely. The children took turns sitting next to him at the table.

Shortly after dinner, Sophie and Rafael left with their children, and Rashid's daughters asked him if he would tell them a story before they went to bed.

"As a matter of fact, I do have a story. A long time ago (as you know, all stories seemed to have happened a long time ago), there were two little girls. They both liked to dream dreams and to share their dreams with each other because they were good friends. One girl was named Jeannie; the other girl was named Rita. They used to dream about what their lives would be like when they grew up to become young ladies.

"Jeannie dreamed about traveling to faraway places, and seeing all the wonderful things in the world, and meeting people in strange countries. Rita was more practical. She dreamed about meeting a very handsome young man, who would be kind and caring, and one day marrying him, and having beautiful children.

" 'But that sounds so boring,' Jeannie said to her.

" 'Not at all. I think it will be a great adventure.'

"When the girls grew older, they could not wait to carry out their dreams. Jeannie went to faraway places and saw all kinds of cities and people of many cultures and nationalities. Jeannie was well liked by all the wonderful people she met.

"Rita also grew to be a very attractive young lady. Because she was kind and caring, she too was very popular and had many friends. There was a student in her class whom she liked very much. They became the best of friends, and soon after graduation, they married. Her husband had no difficulty finding a good job, and Rita and her husband were very happy. The following year a baby was born to them, and they were both thrilled and thanked God every day for this wonderful gift.

"Jeannie finally came home after all her travels and was happy to see her sister and her new brother-in-law and the beautiful little baby, who by now was almost two years old. It was a very happy reunion for everyone. Even though Jeannie was happy for her sister, she could not help but feel a little sad that she did not have a beautiful little child like her sister.

" 'But look at all the places you have seen and all the people you have met,' her sister said to console her. 'You are preparing yourself for what you must do in your life. Though it may be lonely for you and you might miss what I have, you have great things to accomplish in your life.'

"That was little comfort to Jeannie, who could not see the life that stood before her.

"As time passed, however, what her sister told her was true. All her travels and experiences were a preparation for what God had planned for her all along. She eventually did accomplish great things and touched many people's lives by her goodness and unselfish interest in trying to make the world a better place in which to live. But as busy as her life was, there was still a loneliness that made her realize one day that only God could fill that empty place in her heart. That is what finally gave her peace and a love that filled her life with a great joy."

"That is a beautiful story, Joshua," the children told him. They thanked him with hugs and kisses and left to get ready for bed.

"Good night, Joshua!" they called to him as they left the room.

By the time Joshua asked his Father to bless them with a peaceful sleep, they had already run up the stairs.

"Well, you have certainly won their hearts," Rashid said with a broad smile.

"The little ones have such beautiful innocence. Would that they could keep that innocence for a lifetime," Joshua responded.

"I pray they will," Miriam responded as she crossed herself.

After telling the children their story, Joshua spent a few more minutes with Rashid as they decided to schedule the meeting at Ibrahim's house for Thursday of the week following. Of course, that was assuming Ibrahim was agreeable. Joshua already knew he would be, so the meeting was as good as scheduled.

The two men spent the following days contacting all their important friends, telling them of their plans. It was impossible for them to contain their excitement over the possibility that they could do something positive in the frightful climate of hate and self-righteous vindictiveness that was sweeping the country and, indeed, the whole world. Everyone contacted, especially Ibrahim, was willing to drop all other plans to make sure they would be part of this first important meeting.

IN THE MEANTIME, DAN HALLORAN AND TOM CLARK HAD reported to their superior all the information they had gathered and convinced him that they were on to something very suspicious and felt that something big was about to break. They were certain that Ibrahim Abdul was a key figure in whatever was being planned. The information was immediately relayed to the attorney general, who was keenly interested in anything that smelled even remotely suspicious. He ordered that Ibrahim Abdul's house be kept under twenty-four-hour surveillance and that if anything suspicious surfaced, it should be reported to him immediately. They must be ready to move without delay should the occasion arise.

And that occasion did arise, on Thursday of the following week. In the intervening days, Halloran and Clark and others assigned to the case used every means they could to obtain profiles on Joshua, Ibrahim, and Rashid's family members and friends, as well as business contacts and even acquaintances.

When evil or treachery on the part of all these suspects could not be verified by facts, paranoia supplied the necessary justification. With unconcealed glee, the agents made ready to move.

All during Thursday of that following week, they put together a veritable army of federal operatives to close in on the unsuspecting friends of Joshua and Rashid as they gathered at Ibrahim's house for their meeting.

By six-thirty that evening, the whole group arrived. Among them were Arabs of various nationalities as well as concerned Jews of all denominations, over seventy-five persons in all. So enthusiastic were they about their meeting, not one of them was late. The meeting started precisely at seven o'clock. After Ibrahim thanked everyone for coming and expressed his gratitude for including him and especially for the honor of considering his house for the meeting, he asked Joshua to begin with a prayer. Joshua's words were beautiful.

"Father, we approach You with bowed heads and humble hearts, for what we have set out to do is not easy, nor is it within our ability or resources to accomplish, without Your guidance and Your wisdom. We pray You to send Your Spirit to be among us as we lay before You our humble plans to bring peace to our troubled world. All of us who are gathered here this evening, Father, are children of Abraham, representing the many nations You promised Abraham so long ago. Now these chosen few have become one in Your love and offer themselves to bring peace to Your family. They are few, but they are special, Father, and have been chosen because of their goodness and innocence. They will need courage and fortitude, as their enemies are not those whom they might suspect, but the self-righteous who so often see evil where there is only innocence and goodness. I ask You, Father, to give each one here the strength and perseverance we need to carry this noble undertaking to its fulfillment. Bless their families, Father, and keep them in Your care."

"Now, ladies and gentlemen, we begin our work," Ibrahim said as he took over the meeting. "We are honored tonight by the presence of Rabbi Marsha Rapkin. I found out she used to be in the publishing business but now is a full-time rabbi. Thank you for being part of our group. I would like to introduce you to Rashid Abboud, a dear friend whom I have known for years. Although I am a Christian, a Maronite Christian from Lebanon, and Rashid is a Muslim, we have been best of friends for as long as I can remember. Rashid was one of the first to be contacted by Joshua, who inspired this mission, and he is responsible for many of those who are here this evening. Rashid, would you please come up here so everyone can see you and hear you?"

Before Rashid reached the front of the spacious room, which was really a private ballroom, the doors of the three entrances came crashing open and the peaceful calm was destroyed by a small army of federal agents.

"Everyone, stay where you are and no one will get hurt. We are federal agents," the leader said as he extended his identification to Ibrahim. "You are all being detained for questioning. You will be read your rights as you are being escorted into the police vehicles."

At that point, Ibrahim approached the agent in charge and asked what they were all being questioned for.

"You will find that out later. Just do as you are told and no one will get hurt," the officer answered.

Some of the men asked if they could call their wives. "No, there is no need for that. Just proceed outside and you will be told what to do."

In no time at all, the whole group, over seventy-five people in all, were settled in the three vans and a bus that were waiting in the courtyard of the mansion.

"I have never been treated so disgracefully in all my life," Ibrahim said in total disgust as he marched past the officer in charge, "at least not since I was in a Communist country. What has happened to our great country? How fragile are our rights! How fragile even our beloved democracy! I guess it takes only a few sick people to destroy a democracy and strip us of our rights."

The trip to the detention center was tense. "What have we done wrong?" everyone kept asking. But no response was forthcoming. No reading of rights. Technically there was no arrest, so no violation of rights, just the unenlightened behavior of agents of an advanced society.

For some reason, everyone turned to Joshua for understanding, as if he would have the answer. Why Joshua? No one really knew him. Joshua was calm and pensive. He did not seem overly concerned, nor did he even seem surprised. His only response was simple: "Don't be concerned. It will all work out. This is only temporary. It will not frustrate our mission."

His calm settled the near panic of the others.

"How can you feel so certain?" Rashid asked. "Our reputations and businesses are at stake."

"Don't worry. The American people are very reasonable and just. They can see through the paranoia of the politicians. Their sympathy will be for you when this is brought to light. So do not be afraid!"

At the detention center, they were all marched out like prison convicts.

"Humiliating, humiliating," said Ibrahim. "I never would have thought that such a thing could happen to me in America. It shatters my dreams and ideals. They are more like the

Gestapo. No arrest, no lawyer, but imprisoned just the same, without a hearing."

"Be calm, Ibrahim," Joshua said to him quietly. "You will be surprised at the outcome."

"I wish I could share your faith," Ibrahim replied.

"Life is a chess game," Joshua said. "This game has been playing out for weeks now. You have seen just one move. The next move will change things."

Inside the center, each was searched and identified. Then they were led into a large room not unlike a military barracks and told to wait until they were called. They sat on their cots and wondered what would happen next.

The first one called in for interrogation was Rashid. He was the one who seemed closest to Joshua.

"What is your name?" asked the interrogator.

"What have I done that I should be arrested for?"

"I will ask the questions. You just answer."

"My name is Rashid Abboud."

"Where do you live?"

"I live at 815 Spring Street in northwest Washington."

After a long series of routine questions, the interrogator zeroed in on the purpose of the questioning. "Do you know Joshua ben-Youssef?"

"If you mean Joshua, the man who was arrested with us, yes, I do know him, though I do not know his last name. He is a fine young man."

"You have not been *arrested*. You are merely being held for questioning."

"I am sorry. I do not know the difference between being arrested and being locked in a detention center. I am not a lawyer, sir."

"How long have you known Joshua ben-Youssef?"

"For perhaps three, four weeks at most. I met him at our mosque, where I was worshipping at the time."

"You have never known him before?"

"No."

"What transpired between the two of you on that occasion?"

"We greeted each other and he told me he had something very important to share with me. He told me he was Jewish and that he was concerned about all the trouble and anguish between the Arabs and Jews in the Middle East and asked if he could share some of his concerns with me."

"What were those concerns?"

"The hatred and killing on both sides, and the past injustice to the Palestinians."

"Were you interested in what he had to say?"

"Of course I was."

"What did he have to say after that?"

"I invited him to my house, where we had dinner and then we talked."

"About what?"

"More of what he had told me at the mosque."

"Which was?"

"That he would like to gather together others, concerned Jews and Arabs, and try to make some kind of contribution toward peace in the Middle East."

"That was all he discussed with you?"

"That was all we discussed."

"And what did you both decide?"

"That we would both try to find influential people and invite them to form a large group of influential persons who could put pressure on both Israeli and Palestinian leaders to work for peace, and not just talk about it."

"And that is all you talked about?"

"That was it, sir."

All through the night the interrogation continued, with other agents taking over after every few sessions. One after another of the detainees testified to exactly the same thing. Everyone had only good things to say about Joshua. About the purpose of the meeting at Ibrahim's mansion, they all testified that it was to plan on how to contact other people and pressure Arab and Israeli leaders to work for peace. Late into the night, the interrogation became intense and bordered on psychologically torturing the men in an attempt to force them to admit to some evil plot. To a man, no one could offer anything incriminating.

The most interesting of the interrogations involved the Jewish rabbi Marsha Rapkin. She was by no means going to keep her peace. She let her interrogators know, in unambiguous, rapid-fire language, that she felt humiliated, violated, and stripped of her rights not only as a citizen, but as a human being. Furthermore, this was not going to be the end of what she had to say. They would be hearing from her and her lawyers as soon as she was free. When she finished, the agents were sorry they had even interviewed her.

By morning, all the interrogators were exhausted and frustrated. In exchanging notes over what they had collected during all the sessions, they were shocked to find that all the detainees had said practically the same thing. They were hoping they could get information on Joshua, damning information that could be used against him. But the whole night's work produced nothing. This they had to report to their superior, who immediately called the attorney general. His response bordered on rage when what he had hoped would be dramatic evidence of an actual cell of terrorists in the act of plotting a violent event turned out to be nothing more than a group of upstanding citizens trying to make a difference by using their influence for good. The attorney general was even more upset because he had already alerted the news media that he was about to release a story concerning a terrorist plot that he had been able to thwart.

He instructed the agents, "Release the prominent persons you detained, and just hope the reporters don't find out that we arrested people so well respected. However, hold the others for further questioning. Perhaps some of them will break and say what we need to hear to bolster our credibility with the public. After all our beefed-up intelligence gathering for over two years, we have come up with very little to convince the people of an imminent threat of further terrorism."

However, before they had a chance to identify and release Ibrahim and other prominent individuals, angry calls came into the attorney general's office from people high in the government who were outraged that members of their families and families of close friends were being held as terrorist suspects. Embarrassed and confused, the attorney general was at a loss as to how to respond. All he could do was admit that he had depended too much on his staff to do their homework and now realized they had done sloppy investigating and that these were good people guilty of nothing more than wanting to foster a movement for peace in the Middle East. He assured his callers that the detainees would be released as soon as possible, which was just what took place within the next two hours.

Dan Halloran and Tom Clark were summoned to their superior's office and scolded for having stupidly led the agency and the attorney general into such a humiliating predicament. They would all be lucky if they did not lose their jobs or be demoted. After a stinging tongue-lashing, the two men were suspended for two weeks to think over what they had done.

Tom Clark had tried to warn his partner on a number of occasions that they could be making a big mistake, but Halloran, convinced he was on the trail of something big, would not listen. Even after this debacle, he was still determined to pursue his suspicions, even if he had to do it on his own time. His connections in the agency, and in other high places, allowed him more license than would be tolerated in another agent.

It was only a matter of minutes before the news media descended on the attorney general's office, too impatient to wait for his call. There was no way they were going to miss this dramatic story. The spokeswoman for the agency assured them that as soon as the attorney general had all his information, he would certainly contact them.

While they were still questioning the spokeswoman, one of the female journalists received an urgent message from a reporter at the detention center telling her that a whole crowd of people had just been released from detention and that journalists at the scene were busy interviewing everyone involved. The agents were not available for comment, but the people were more than willing to reveal the grueling details of their nightmare. Recognizing some of them as prominent Washington businessmen, the reporters were shocked to find that they had been taken in and detained. There must have been a major blunder somewhere and by someone.

The radio, television, and newspapers all carried the story, which made the attorney general look as if, in his desperate need to arrest somebody with genuine terrorist credentials, he had made a major gaffe in arresting not only ordinary decent citizens, but citizens prominent in the community as well, some internationally prominent. They were all people whose only crime was that they were of Middle Eastern descent and were trying to see how they could use their considerable influence to help stop the violence in the Holy Land. Among those arrested and detained was a female Jewish rabbi, who merely wanted to lend her support to promote peace in her family's homeland.

As the two agents were psychologically unable to accept responsibility for such a humiliating incident, they naturally blamed Joshua for everything that had happened. They were more determined than ever to find something that would incriminate him. Having other colleagues of like mind who relished pursuing conspiracy theories, they had no trouble eliciting their volunteer help in tracking Joshua with their state-of-the-art surveillance equipment, which of course was no match for Joshua's superior information-gathering techniques. He was fully aware of what he was up against. All he did was smile as he realized what they were planning.

During the time the group was still in the detention center, their families found out from Ibrahim's wife, Cynthia, what had happened. Panic and fear gripped them all, especially the little children. Rashid's family was most upset because they had so many relatives nearby. Late in the evening, just as the children had gone to sleep and while Miriam was praying by her bedside, she was disturbed by a strange presence in her room. At first it was just a feeling; then, above her bed, a soft light appeared and a beautiful woman stood before her, with dark hair and dark eyes, no different from any Middle Eastern woman, and with a long robe like the kind worn by women in the Middle East. Miriam was not frightened. On the contrary, she felt a peacefulness that she could not understand.

"Do not be afraid, Miriam. I have come to bring you peace."

"Who are you?" she asked.

"My name is like yours. I am Miriam, Jesus' mother."

The lady said only a few words: "My son sent me to you. Do not be afraid. All will be well. Tell the others, especially the children. I know how troubled they are, and I feel their pain. But tell them not to worry and that all will be well!" Then she vanished as discreetly as she had appeared.

Miriam did feel at peace. The panic, the fear, the terrible anxiety of not knowing—it all dissolved as calm serenity bathed her heart in a gentle tranquillity.

7

THE FBI RELEASED THE GROUP OUT INTO THE STREET without so much as an apology. They were far from their homes, so they had to contact their families to come and pick them up. No one could believe this had happened to them. They were all good citizens and in good standing with the government. They had never caused any trouble. It was like a nightmare come to life. A few of the people involved lost their nerve and backed out of the project, but most were more determined than ever to carry out their plan. By day's end, they had contacted one another and called Ibrahim to reschedule their aborted meeting.

"If you can all make it, I would be happy to have you over tomorrow evening, so we can get this thing started," was his determined response. "In fact, come early and we'll have a nice buffet all set up for you, so we can enjoy our evening."

When everyone arrived home, they were greeted with tears and hugs and emotional expressions of relief. Miriam could not wait to tell Rashid of the special visitor who had come to comfort her the previous night. She also told him that the visitor told her she was the Blessed Mother and that she should tell the other families that they would all be freed and that no harm would come to them. Rashid was not very impressed and gave it little heed.

The next evening came fast. Everyone arrived at Ibrahim's in plenty of time, as all were eager to spend at least a few minutes with their host, whom many people admired and respected from a distance but had never had the honor of talking to personally. As important a person as he was, he was gracious to every guest, making each feel as if he were the one who was being honored. A very rare man indeed!

The seats were arranged less formally than at their previous attempt at a meeting, in little more than a half circle, with a large table full of good things to eat in the open area. This way, the discussions could take place even as people wandered over to the table for further helpings if they so chose. It was a pleasant evening and profitable as well. It was decided that Ibrahim would contact his most influential friends in Lebanon who had contacts with Palestinians and inform them of their plans. Rabbi Rapkin would contact an influential group of Orthodox Jews and other concerned Jews, inform them of the project, and elicit their support. The other members would contact their friends locally and nationwide and get them involved. Those who had contacts in other countries would make them aware of their plans and ask their help as well, assuring all that the whole plan would be aboveboard and executed very discreetly so there could be no misunderstanding or suspicion of anything illegal or devious.

For answers, they would have to wait almost two weeks before everyone responded. When the responses did come, they were overwhelmingly positive, though some felt uncomfortable, fearing that, in the present circumstances where they lived, their families might be put in a difficult situation.

There were enough positive responses, however, to reassure all involved that a powerful network could be developed. Some of the foreign contacts were indeed people of great influence. Among them were two princes in Saudi Arabia, a wealthy banker in Bahrain, export-import people in Lebanon, a private secretary to the president of Syria as well as two wealthy lawyer-businessmen in that country, and a personal friend of the prime minister of Iran. All these people agreed that they would be willing to do whatever they could to lend support to the project.

Rabbi Rapkin's contacts were not as well placed, but some of those who responded to her had important and highly placed contacts in Israel. They would contact them and ask their help, which they were sure would be forthcoming.

Joshua did not have the contacts the others had, but his value was in his ability to share with the group his ideas for developing a workable strategy once everyone was on board. At the next meeting, everyone was impatient to share their success in getting others to commit to the project. They were all off to a good start.

Ibrahim asked Joshua if he would preside at the meeting and share with everyone how he saw the project developing and what their next move should be.

"Thank you, Ibrahim. I would like to express my admiration to all of you for the dignity with which you conducted yourselves during our recent unpleasant experience. I assure you that no matter what obstacles may come up, we will pass through them untouched, so do not be afraid. This project is so important, there will be other attempts to stall it, and even to destroy our efforts, but still do not be afraid. Nothing will touch you. The Evil One can only frighten you, but not destroy you. My Father does not give him that power. He has power only to play tricks, but that is all, so don't be afraid.

"The next move? What should that be? First of all, it is important that all those people you contacted locally and in other places in the country should come to Washington and meet with us, so we can all become acquainted with one another and share our plans. It is important that they all feel comfortable with what we are doing so they can be wholehearted in their support. It is also important that on Ibrahim's next visit to the Middle East he meet with all the people you have contacted over there. Perhaps he could take a few of you with him so you can introduce him to your friends in those areas. Some will be Jews, some will be Arabs. They are all the children of Abraham. He is not the father of one nation. He is the father of many nations, and it breaks my Father's heart to see Abraham's children destroying one another. The slaughter at Shatila was especially offensive to my Father, as is the murdering of innocent people that is still taking place. As a final goal, nothing would make my Father happier than to see all His children worshipping together on the Temple Mount and sharing the Holy City as brothers and sisters. What pleasure could my Father have in prayers offered in a place that drips with the blood of innocent people? Prayers offered to God on the Temple Mount will be acceptable only when all His children are free to gather there and worship together. For this we can all pray.

"Good people on both sides want this fratricide to stop. Your friends there can be of great help in gathering the good people together. Ibrahim can share with them the plans we decide on here and also set up channels of rapid communication so they can be kept up-to-date in all matters we discuss and also so they can share with us their progress. One of the long-range plans that we have to keep in the back of our minds is that economic development among Palestinians has to be a priority. Another long-range plan has to be entrée for Israeli businesses to markets in Arab countries. These two goals have to have top priority ultimately. It is important and critical that Israelis and Arabs form their own economic bloc that is self-supporting and capable of growing to its full potential eventually. There is no reason why Israelis and Arabs have to be dependent on any other outside countries for economic support. They have resources enough of every kind to assure them independence in the future, if they can decide to work together and not destroy each other.

"What I have just described to you is the plan in brief. It will become more fully developed as we take each step. For the present that is all we need see. The rest will unfold as the time is ready."

Rashid was the first to respond to Joshua's talk. "Joshua, you are usually so quiet and unassuming, I would never have imagined you could stand before an audience like this and be so self-assured and give such a masterful delivery of a vision so profound and comprehensive, in a way that you make sound so simple and understandable. Your own simple bearing belies the genius you keep so well hidden. The plan you have just outlined is something we can all become very passionate about. I am sure when it is presented to our friends abroad and they discuss it with their contacts on both sides in the Holy Land, there will be among them much to think about and mull over in their quiet moments. It is the only way. To a reasonable mind, it has to be the only way. They all must learn to forget themselves and their petty hatreds and think of the future—not their own future, but the future of their children and their grandchildren. If they concentrate on that, they will see their way clear to doing the right thing."

Rabbi Rapkin stood and asked if she could say a few words.

"Of course," Ibrahim responded. "You are all free to speak."

"I cannot tell you how happy I am to have been invited to be part of this wonderful project. I feel very close to all of you, especially since we have been prison inmates together. I know I do not have the contacts you all have, but I just want to let you all know that if there is anything I can do in my own limited way, I will be ready to help in whatever way I can. Please feel free to call at any time. I do have friends, Jewish friends, in Brooklyn, Orthodox, some of them rabbis, who are very unhappy with radical Israeli politicians and their supporters. They have already expressed deep interest in what we are undertaking. I also have some friends in high places in Israel and a few relatives living in a kibbutz in Israel. They have always been very close. Perhaps they might even be willing to help in some small way. They have important contacts over there. Some have already expressed their willingness to work with us. Again, thank you for inviting me to be with you."

"Thank you, Rabbi," Ibrahim responded. "You are a brave woman. We are proud to have you as part of our group."

After other brief discussions, and deciding to meet again in two weeks, Ibrahim ended the meeting. As everyone was leaving, he asked Joshua if he would honor him by staying at his house that evening. He had many things he wanted to discuss with him. Joshua was happy for the invitation, as it was a chilly night.

Joshua slept soundly that night in a comfortable bed, the kind they never had in days long past. He arose at sunrise and walked quietly out into the garden. He wondered if the family ever took the time to wander through the paths of the beautiful garden, with its flowers of every color and description. The busy life of important people rarely allows for quiet meditation. Joshua's life was busy, but spending time with his Father was an important part of his life. The Father and he were one, really one, in everything. They shared and planned and made decisions that affected the life of the universe all day long. These few moments of peace before the others arose were a treasure, a rare luxury in the midst of all the busyness of living among humans. Resting in the garden with the colorful, fragrant flowers in the presence of his Father and the Spirit of Wisdom and Love was the nearest thing to being in heaven. People should take time to appreciate these simple pleasures. They are so healing.

In the midst of his reveries, Ibrahim quietly walked up to him, so as not to break his mood.

"Joshua, enjoying the peace and quiet of my garden?" he asked.

"Yes, it is so restful and soothing to walk through such beauty."

"I know. I wish I spent more time in my garden. I do work in it occasionally, but not nearly as much as I should. I should just come out and enjoy it sometimes. Unfortunately, we get caught up in all our work and forget the good things that are all around us. I am going to promise myself that I will spend more time enjoying God's gifts."

"Thank you, friend, for the invitation to sleep in that wonderfully comfortable bed. I slept well, and only when the sun rose and shone through my window did I wake up. What a peaceful, restful sleep."

"I am just happy you stayed. It was really for a very selfish motive that I asked you. There are some personal matters that

I was hoping to discuss with you this morning, if you don't mind."

"Not at all. Working on people's personal matters has always been part of my life, an enjoyable part, I might say."

"I am glad you don't mind," Ibrahim said. "It is not so much a problem I want to discuss, but nonetheless a matter of deep concern. I have a cousin who was an officer in the Lebanese militia. He is a Christian. When the Palestinian women and children were herded into the refugee camp at Shatila, and Sharon had sealed off the exits and given the signal to the militia, my cousin was one of the officers responsible for the massacre of those women and children, almost a thousand of them. Our family has always been so close, I cannot help but feel partly responsible for that massacre. It is a horrible black mark on our family's conscience. We all feel the guilt, although we had no personal part in what happened that day. I felt even more shame when the United States refused to condemn the massacre. As an Arab, I feel such guilt and such conflicting feelings. As a loyal American, I feel doubly troubled that our country does not understand how the Palestinians have been brutalized for so long and does nothing to bring justice to both sides. As an Arab, I feel guilty over suicide bombers killing innocent Israelis. Joshua, I have never been so mixed up in my life. I used to have it all together, but now I have many sleepless nights."

"Ibrahim, step outside yourself for a moment and detach yourself from what you just told me. A young boy has just told you that he has a brother who belonged to a gang. A short time ago, that brother had killed an innocent man while robbing his store. The boy told you that he felt terrible guilt over what his brother had done. What would you tell that boy?"

"I would have to tell him that he had no reason to feel guilty. He had nothing to do with what his brother had done. Nor did he encourage him in any way. I would also tell him that he has no responsibility whatsoever. Joshua, I can, however, understand his shame, because of the black mark on his family's conscience. But the boy would also wonder if he could not have done more for his brother to prevent him from going down that path. The boy is confusing shame with guilt. I would tell him his own goodness could restore the family's good name. Ah, Joshua, I think I understand what you are telling me. But it is not easy. I will still go through life suffering the pain."

"Friend, I know it is not easy, but the guilt is not yours. Should God feel guilty for having given free will to all the people who abuse that freedom by doing evil things? You feel shame because your cousin is a part of you. Pray to my Father. Plead with Him to bring those innocent victims home to heaven and comfort the hearts of the families who have lost them. My Father will hear you and He will make up for the hurt and the anguish. Pray each day, and bring your prayers before my Father. You will one day see how wonderfully He answers your prayers. He can also heal our troubled memories."

"I wish God was as real to me as He is to you, Joshua. You call Him Father as if you really know Him and feel an intimacy with Him. I wish I could feel that way."

"In time, in time, my friend. Now you can be at peace, knowing that my Father, and your Father, too, will be your partner in healing the wounds of those who suffer."

"Thank you. I feel much better. Shall we go in for breakfast? I hope you don't mind a real Arab or Jewish breakfast."

"Not at all. It's been a long time since I had a breakfast like that."

ALTHOUGH THEY WERE FREED FROM DETENTION, Joshua's friends were far from free. They were under constant surveillance. Business associates and friends were harassed, questioned constantly about every detail in their private lives, raising suspicions and fears over their own associations with people under investigation by government officials. So many of these officials were good people, but they were haunted by an obsession with possible terrorist attacks from within their own communities. Joshua could not help but reminisce over how little things had changed and how alike people are after so many centuries. It may be a long time since the days of the scribes and Pharisees, and the spies they sent to monitor his every move, but there is still that same uneasiness and suspicion about his behavior and values. Innocent goodness is presumed specious until proven otherwise, as if real goodness is too good to be believable—or perhaps, which is more likely, meanness and arrogance are shamed by the mere presence of innocence and goodness. Today in our civilized and highly educated world, Jesus' values and his vision are either simplistic and ridiculed or suspect and avoided as traps to ensnare the unwary. His concept of love and forgiveness is sneered at by those who cannot lay aside their need to hate, to punish, and to seek retribution. His actions when performed, even vicariously through his followers who have imbibed his spirit, are monitored and reported to authorities and often punished as dangerous and possibly subversive of the public good. How many saintly American and Dutch priests and nuns were assassinated in Central and South America with the tacit approval of our government? What was their crime? They tried to educate the poor and teach them how to earn a living and rise out of their poverty. To educate the poor was subversive. To teach them how to work and live independently was a crime. It threatened the rich and the powerful, who had kept them in abject poverty and ignorance for three hundred years. This had been the only way to control the masses and prevent rebellion. Keeping them poor, without resources, and ignorant was the best assurance of permanent domination. Trying to educate them and better their lives, as saintly missionaries have done, is a crime punishable by assassination. Jesus' message was one of freedom and liberation from domination. Those who preached that message were dangerous. Teaching personal dignity and independence could not be tolerated.

One of Ibrahim's friends who had been detained with the group believed strongly in what Jesus taught, especially his concern for the poor. He belonged to an old and loyal Christian family that had originally come from Iran and emigrated to the United States many years ago. The man's name was Elie Zambaka. Though a shrewd businessman, on Sunday mornings after Mass he would go to the local deli and buy large trays of sandwiches and coffee and bring them down to places where the homeless gathered. Each Sunday morning saw more and more homeless waiting for him. Elie smiled when he realized how much his little gesture meant to them. His first concern when he was detained was who would take care of the homeless should he still be in jail on the following Sunday.

Joshua had become particularly close to Elie, as he understood the pain and loneliness of a soul so sensitive. Two days after the meeting at Ibrahim's house, Elie invited Joshua to his apartment, which was in Silver Spring. He had many things to share with him and wanted Joshua to be his friend, as he always felt very much alone. It was not that he was alone, because his family loved him deeply and kept a warm and close relationship with him. They were always there when he needed them, and that care and concern were reciprocated. His young nephews particularly were fond of him, and he loved them dearly and brought them into his business as they grew old enough. Little Richard was his best friend. His two sisters, Joan and Mathilde, were not just sisters, but also dear friends, as were their husbands. It was a beautiful family, sometimes too close, perhaps, but better that than the unhealthy coldness and distance of so many families whose members rarely talk to one another. Their family reminded Joshua of Mary, Martha, and Lazarus, whom he visited so often in the distant past. Those memories were still fresh and brought a twinge of nostalgia as he thought of them. I never realized so fully the joy and the pain of being human as I did in those days, he thought. Since then I can feel the bewilderment of being human and how difficult is a simple life when there are so many pressures and fears that invade an innocent soul.

Elie was one of those innocent souls, confused by the complexities of a world that was too far beyond his comprehension, a world that mystified him and made him feel as if he did not belong. He was in his inner self the citizen of another world, the world that Joshua would call home. The two were instinctively drawn to each other. When Elie talked to him, he laid bare his soul. Joshua was the only one he could trust to share so much. He rarely revealed anything of himself even to his dearest friends, who loved him very much. It seemed once he found Joshua, he became his only true friend. He knew Joshua understood him and accepted him as he was, with all his failings. In fact, it was as if Joshua overlooked his failings. Instead, he tried to make him appreciate the good he possessed and his personal worth, which Elie could never see or would not allow himself to see.

Elie and Ibrahim were business associates. Ibrahim needed Elie for his contacts in Iran, as Ibrahim knew no Farsi, which Elie spoke fluently. Their relationship started out as a business arrangement but soon developed into a personal friendship, as they shared much in common—their ideas, their faith, their concern for the poor—besides their shrewd instinct for business.

In this latest project, Ibrahim needed Elie's advice and access to his friends in the Middle East. The two would spend much time together at Ibrahim's house as they planned their strategy.

"Elie, who are your most important contacts in Jordan, in the Holy Land, and in Syria?" Ibrahim asked him point-blank.

"Dear friend," Elie shot back, surprised at the bluntness of the question, "my most important contacts? You catch me off guard. I am reluctant to share them with anyone. I have kept their cover for years and deal with them directly when I have to. They are key players in activities in the region and would not be particularly impressed if I betrayed their identity, even to you, although some of them already know you. If you share with me what you want them to know, I would be happy to communicate it to them. From then on, they can either contact you or relay their response back to me and I can tell you."

"I understand," Ibrahim responded. "Anonymity is essential these days. But it is important for us to know just where we can contact these people concerning matters we might discuss with them in the near future. And we have to know that they can be trusted. If just one person is opposed to what we are doing, he could undermine everything before it even gets started."

"Well, if it's any comfort, I have talked to them about these things often, and they are just where we are, but they are concerned about support. Would there be outside support? That is their worry. They listen to the Iranian-language radio station in California, and that encourages them, but they need to be assured of solid, concrete support."

"Good, then we have a place to start. Can you contact them tonight?"

"Their time or our time?" Elie asked.

"Their time."

"It's as good as done. I'll have the information tomorrow morning by two a.m."

Over his loud belly laugh, Ibrahim warned him, "It can wait till breakfast. Before I have my Arabic coffee I am brain-dead."

Elie wasted no time. He was a high-energy person, and once in high gear no one could keep up with him. By two a.m., he had all the information needed and enthusiastic commitments besides. He was tempted to call Ibrahim but thought better of it and went to bed to catch a few hours' sleep.

"Good morning, Mrs. Abdul! Is Ibrahim available?"

"Good morning, Elie! He will be alive in a minute. I just gave him his coffee. Will you be honoring us with your presence for breakfast? We would both love to have you with us."

"If it would not be an imposition."

"Never. We'll be expecting you in a few minutes. We'll have your favorite."

Elie was there before Ibrahim finished his Arabic coffee.

"If you had come two minutes earlier, you would not have been welcome," Ibrahim told him as he entered the kitchen.

"Ibrahim, how can you talk to a dear friend like that?" Cynthia, his wife, said to him. "You should be ashamed of yourself."

"Well, it's true. I told him not to call before I had my coffee. Don't give him any. He's hyper enough."

"How can you be so insulting?" Cynthia said, scolding him a second time. "Look at him! He takes your insults so graciously. Elie, don't pay attention to him. That's his early morning humor. It took me years to get used to it. Sit down here and we'll all have a nice quiet, peaceful breakfast, won't we, dear?"

Ibrahim grunted what was assumed to be agreement, and Cynthia brought from the stove a platter of ham and eggs and crispy rice, which she knew Elie loved.

"Cynthia, you are such a sweetheart! My favorite, crispy rice. Thank you so much. If you don't mind, I will take some Arabic coffee, in spite of what the grump said."

Ibrahim even poured it for him, and they all settled down to their business breakfast, of which Cynthia was an active partner.

"Well, what did you find?" Ibrahim asked, showing more signs of life.

"Plenty. Wait till you hear what I've learned," Elie replied excitedly.

"Tell me!"

"One contact I can let you know about is one of my friends, a Palestinian by the name of Ali Messawari, a key person in Hamas. He used to be a real radical, but recently one of his kids got killed in a suicide bombing. He had tried to keep him out of it. Since then his whole world has fallen apart and he's had a total change of heart. He had such high hopes for that boy. He finally realized the futility of Palestinians killing their own children just to prove a point. Peace has to come eventually whether the kids commit suicide or not. What they're doing now is wasting innocent children just to feed their hate. Those kids could one day have been the leaders of the people. So, bottom line is, he is willing to do what he can to change the others. He'll be with us if we can come up with the support."

"That's amazing."

"That's not all. Another contact who was a friend when we were living in Iran is an ayatollah. His name is Saladin Reza. He is a brilliant man, educated in the United States, and has degrees in philosophy and mathematics. He is also a university professor, living in Saudi Arabia. He said he is willing to form a peace movement among a coalition of Sunni and Shiite Muslims. He has many friends in both camps. His family is also very influential and extremely wealthy and will support him. He promised to contact Messawari and offer help and considerable funding for Hamas leaders if they desist from the use of violence. The funding will be used to help build up the economy."

"Elie, I can't believe you have done all this since yesterday."

"You have to understand, Ibrahim, that these thoughts are not new to them. They have been dreaming about something like this for years, and knowing that there are reputable and practical people sponsoring this whole thing is just what they have been hoping for. They have been ready for a long time and are only too willing to be a part of it.

"And that is not all. I talked to Rabbi Rapkin and asked if she has any friends, important friends, in Israel. She gave me a list. Some are just ordinary people, although they're important, too. But she gave me the names of two very important businessmen in Haifa. She already spoke to them over a week ago. After she explained what we were planning, and mentioned your name and the names of some of the others, they were willing to help in whatever way they could. They thought they could help later on, by forming business partnerships with you and some of your Arab friends in that area, the beginning of a solid economic bloc of Arabs and Israelis."

"You sound like Joshua," Ibrahim said with a smile. "For a saintly, spiritual man, Joshua can be very earthy."

"Realistic is a better word," Elie replied. "He knows that those people will never come together for spiritual motives and that economics is the only motive that will move them over the long term, after security issues are resolved. Joshua had a great idea in suggesting that we involve people over there who are close to the problem rather than foreigners working from the outside. Only those involved can make peace, and as Joshua told me one day, 'It has to come from their hearts. Once they think of their children and their grandchildren rather than their hatred, they will make the sacrifices necessary for peace. The Father cannot give that kind of peace. He can give peace to a searching heart, but not to a heart full of hatred.' With all our friends and business contacts working together over there, I think we have a chance. I'm beginning to feel this project can actually work."

"I can't believe you accomplished all this overnight, Elie," Cynthia said in amazement. "Ibrahim, how will you get all this machinery to start working?"

"I have been pondering that problem for a long time. There has to be coordination. Someone will have to be the courier who speaks the languages and can run from one group to another, keeping everyone informed of the progress that all the others are making. This way there will be no slipups. I have been hesitant to ask, but there is only one person who has the skill and ability to speak in all the languages with all the contacts. Elie, would you be willing to do that? It will be dangerous, so don't hesitate to say no if you think it is too much to ask."

There was a long silence as Elie tried to get over the shock and pondered the ramifications of the task—not an easy one, to say the least, and dangerous to the extreme. Arab fanatics would consider him an enemy undermining their vow to destroy Israel. Jewish fanatics would feel the same way. Others might look upon him as a spy. Only his friends would know they could trust him. But someone had to do it. He spoke all the languages needed for the mission. He could talk his way out of even the most compromising situation. He was a born diplomat. There was really no one else.

"Ibrahim, you have had this in your mind for a long time, haven't you. This didn't just come to you all of a sudden as we're sitting here having breakfast. But, yes, I will do it. Give me a few days to get all my affairs in order, as only God knows what the future might bring."

Cynthia felt a powerful premonition over what could happen in those chaotic situations with so many crazy people over there. Her sadness showed on her face as tears began to trickle down her cheeks.

"Someone has to go," her husband said almost apologetically. "Elie is the only one who has the qualifications for such a difficult mission. He speaks all the languages and has more contacts than I do. If he can pull it off, he will be the instrument of God in bringing hope of new life to all those people. We will give him all the support we can and alert our friends to make everyone else over there aware of Elie's mission, so it will be understood right from the beginning."

Elie left with a heavy heart, feeling that this was a mission he might not survive. He needed to talk to Joshua, so as soon as he left he tried to track him down. But that proved unnecessary, as Joshua was waiting outside his house when he arrived home.

"What are you doing here?" Elie asked in surprise.

"I guess I knew you needed to talk. Not much escapes my attention, especially things that concern my friends."

"Shall we go in the house or over to the park?" Elie asked him.

"Let's go over to the park. It is a beautiful day, and we can sit and talk in peace, with no phone calls."

"Good, hop in and we'll drive over. We should be able to find a parking place over there."

As they drove off, Joshua was fully aware that they were being followed. Noticing that Elie kept looking at the rearview mirror, he told him, "Don't be concerned. They follow me everywhere, but my surveillance system is much more efficient than theirs, so I'm always way ahead of them. Just keep driving. I lead them into situations that trick them into drawing conclusions that will eventually backfire on them. Don't be anxious about it. They're harmless."

"You enjoy this, don't you," Elie said with a loud laugh.

"Yes, I do. Why take them seriously when what we are doing is so innocent? Most of those agents are decent, sincere family people, but the handful of arrogant, ambitious ones who think nothing of destroying innocent lives to get a promotion dishonor all the good ones. On the surface they look righteous, but inside they are dangerous. So yes, I play their game, and since I know beforehand each step they take, I think you will enjoy the outcome."

And the outcome was not long in coming.

T HE TWO AGENTS DOGGEDLY TRACKED JOSHUA'S EVERY
move. They now had the use of a van loaded with the
latest surveillance equipment, with specialists to operate each
device. Since no one could conveniently pin a microphone on
Joshua's person, a device was equipped with a camera sensitive
enough to capture the slightest movement of his lips and facial
expressions. Another device could read his lips and interpret
what he was saying—if he spoke in English, of course. As
Joshua sensed immediately what was happening, he spoke to
Elie in Arabic. This totally frustrated the agents.

"This man is uncanny," Dan Halloran said to his partner.
"He seems to know every move we make or are going to make.
Yet he has no electronic devices. How does he know what we
are doing? Do you think he's psychic?"

"You're the one who wants to pursue this," his partner responded. "I'm just going along for the ride, because I'm your
partner. If you didn't have such highly placed friends, I'd have

gotten out of this long ago. So now the next move is yours. But you had better not slip up. Embarrass the boss once more and we're both out of a job."

"But I *know* he's up to something. Why would he start speaking another language as soon as we turn on the device?"

"For a very simple reason—the other guy doesn't know English or doesn't speak it well enough. Maybe he's got what some people call 'the gift of tongues.' How would I know? You're the genius. But whatever it is, the next move is yours. I still think this is all going to backfire and end up putting us in a very embarrassing position, making us look like damn fools. It's as if he's playing a game with us. To me he looks innocent and could have the most innocent of intentions, as suspicious as it may look to someone who sees conspiracies around every corner."

Elie and Joshua went to the park and sat and talked for almost an hour. Elie was deeply troubled over what he had agreed to, but he knew he had to do it. He poured his heart out to Joshua. One of the things he was concerned about was the state of his soul. "Joshua, do you think God holds all our mistakes against us?"

"Elie, do you think I hold your mistakes against you?"

"No."

"Then you don't have to worry about God holding grudges against you for mistakes you made."

"Yes, but you're not God."

"Elie, as long as we've been friends, do you still not know that I reflect the Father in all things? When you know that I do not hold your mistakes against you, you have the assurance my Father does not, either. Just believe me."

"I have a strange premonition that I am not going to survive this mission, that's why I worry about meeting God."

"When you were a little boy, were you afraid to come home from school to see your mother?"

"No, I always knew she would understand no matter what happened."

"Well, the Father is more understanding than all the mothers on earth. Do not be afraid of dying, Elie. Fear of that will make the mission unbearable. Just trust God, and know that you will be doing His work, to help bring His peace to the earth. You will not go home until all your work in this world is finished."

"Joshua, every time I talk to you I feel at peace. Thanks."

"You're my friend, remember. I will always be with you, no matter where you are."

When they finished talking, Elie invited Joshua to lunch at a local deli, after which they parted.

For the next few days, Joshua was nowhere to be found. Then, on Saturday morning, he showed up at the synagogue for services. Agents had been watching the place since early morning and were proud of themselves when he showed up. They were finally right about something. What now befuddled them was the identity of the woman accompanying him to the services. The agents could not help being struck by her extraordinary, flawless beauty, not a glamorous Hollywood beauty, but a beauty that radiated warmth, goodness, compassion. As she smiled at each person she and Joshua met, one could sense she knew each one personally, and their eyes followed her as she passed, wondering how she knew them.

When they approached the entrance, Rabbi Rapkin met them and welcomed them both.

"Rabbi, this is my mother, Miriam," Joshua said with great pride. "And Mother, this is Rabbi Marsha Rapkin, a dear friend."

Miriam smiled and opened her arms as the rabbi reached out to give her a welcoming hug. Together they walked into the sanctuary, where, not wanting to be obvious, Joshua and his mother took seats in the last row.

The conversation was picked up by the recorder in the agents' van, which was parked not far from the entrance to the synagogue. "That woman is his *mother*? God, she's beautiful, and if that's really her son, she looks a lot younger than he does. He looks young enough, but I get a strange feeling he's way older than he looks. This is getting more eerie all the time. Are you sure you still want to pursue this?" Tom commented.

"I'm determined to see this to the end," Dan shot back. "Don't fink out on me. We've gone this far already. We're not backing down now."

"I still think we're making a big mistake."

In the meantime, Rabbi Rapkin went to the microphone, welcomed all the unfamiliar faces, and introduced Miriam as Joshua's mother. Miriam stood briefly and smiled.

The rabbi continued, "I could not help but notice when I was introduced to her how much younger she looks than her son. I guess Joshua never gave her any trouble or cause for anxiety."

Miriam looked at her son and smiled. "If she only knew!"

Joshua chuckled. "In spite of it, Mother, you still look young. Not many mothers have sons who are older than their mothers."

The agents quietly walked into the back of the synagogue, careful not to be noticed by the rabbi this time. They could not cope with another drubbing, especially since the detention, now that everyone knew who was responsible. But Marsha Rapkin noticed them as soon as they came through the door.

"Oh, my! We *do* have some *very* interesting visitors again this morning. Would you two gentlemen who just walked in please make yourselves welcome. It is so nice of you to come back again after your last visit. I am glad you still feel at home with us."

As the agents sheepishly took seats near the rear, the rabbi knew this was her chance. "I must tell you all that these two men are outstanding citizens, true patriots. Though they did not identify themselves during their last visit, I have learned much about them since. Mr. Halloran and Mr. Clark are men of whom our government must be most proud. They are true citizens, completely dedicated to keeping our country free of undesirables.

"I am sure they are men of deep religious faith, and it is that faith that brings them here to worship with us this morning. They sure do our country proud."

By that time, the whole congregation had turned to look at the two men, who had turned crimson as they all clapped, not at the men's patriotism, but at Rabbi Rapkin's chutzpah.

After a few remarks by the president of the synagogue, Rabbi Rapkin went to the microphone again and spoke briefly about the dangers facing America, not least of which was the problem of people who were patriotic to the point where everyone else's patriotism becomes suspect. "The great danger we face is not so much from terrorists as from some of our own people who are obsessed with fear and find threats and conspiracies behind every door. More people's reputations have been ruined and families destroyed by fanatic officials than by the evil done by terrorists. Don't misunderstand me, I know we are under siege by terrorists who hate us, and we must be on our guard continually, but there is a breed of people spawned by our national tragedy who find reason to be suspicious of even the most honest of citizens. They are a real threat to all of us.

"This morning I had intended to speak about forgiveness of those who hurt us, but I guess I blew that one. However, I feel God has His ways, and as our president was speaking, I was thinking about our recent traumatic ordeal, and about Joshua. I have known him for only a short time, but during that time I have come to respect him deeply. I know he has a message for all of us, and I hope he will not be too embarrassed if I ask him to come up to the microphone and speak to us this morning."

All eyes turned and looked for Joshua, who realized that this was going to happen.

"Do you know what you are going to say, son?" his mother asked with a smile.

"Say a prayer I think of something," he said with a broad grin as he rose from the seat and approached the platform. Walking over to the microphone, he smiled at Rabbi Rapkin and told her very quietly, "Just wait! One day, when you least expect it, it will be my turn."

The rabbi smiled, knowing he meant it.

"My friends," Joshua began, "I cannot tell you how much at home I feel with all of you here today. Most of you do not know me very well, except for those who call my name but do not know me. The synagogue has always been home to me, and I wish it were true today.

"Good people today are very frightened. Children are even more frightened at what lies before them. They see grown-ups filled with fear, and they then begin to have sleepless nights and nightmares. People thought this could never happen in America, though people in other countries who once thought the same thing now have endless nightmares, especially the kind that happen in the daylight, nightmares that are only too real, undermining people's will to live. So many feel there is no real purpose to life, as there is no hope for their children. Where there is no hope for the children, what reason is there to bear the daily agony of living? The feeling of hopelessness spreads like a disease.

"That is sad, because people should never allow themselves to lose hope. There is always reason to hope, a reason that is founded on the solid rock of our Father's love. Some may think that fantasy and against common sense. But I know it is real. Let me tell you a parable, a particular parable that is a true story. Many years ago, a famous Jewish writer was hunted by the Gestapo. They had him surrounded and trapped at the famous shrine at Lourdes in France. There was no escape. Looking up at the image of Jesus' mother, he pleaded with her to help him. He even vowed to write the story of how that famous shrine came to be. Bravely trusting that Jesus' mother would protect him, he walked straight past the soldiers and out of the shrine to safety. He kept his vow and years later went back to France, searched the archives of century-old newspapers, and wrote an accurate account of what happened there in his famous book, *The Song of Bernadette*.

"We live in troubled times, times with which people in this country are mostly unfamiliar. Faith in God, and trust in an unseen God seems to many unreasonable. So even those who look upon themselves as people of faith would still rather trust in wars and killing than trust in a loving, caring Father in heaven. But I tell you, do not be afraid to trust. War is never a solution. It is the trigger for greater and more horrible evils. Hatreds caused by wars fester and spread their poison in the souls of humans more viciously than the worst weapons of biological warfare, destroying not only the enemy, but the souls of innocent warriors who thought they were saving the world. Hatred unleashed by war is the most virulent weapon of mass destruction.

"It is only a humble dedication to your Father in heaven and trust in His power and goodness that can save the world today. Do not be ashamed to pray! When my Father sees His children praying together, especially when people of different faiths gather in prayer, those prayers are surely answered. Did not Communism in Russia disappear overnight, and without a war? There are some who will scoff. There are others who say it is unconstitutional to pray to God in public assemblies, but it is important that leaders as well as people express their humble recognition of God and their need for God's saving love. If God were the fiction of some people's minds, that would be different. But God is not a fiction. He is the Creator of you all, and every people owes Him homage. No one should be offended by seeing others in prayer, especially in time of crisis. It does not make sense to be offended by others praying. Pray particularly for the success of the work that your rabbi and all our friends have begun in our attempt to encourage peace among the warring peoples of the Middle East. I am grateful to Rabbi Rapkin for asking me to speak to you this morning. It has been many years since I was at home in a synagogue, and you have made me feel so very much at home here in your beautiful synagogue. May my Father bless you with His choicest graces."

The people seemed to like what Joshua had to say. Most of the congregation knew him only from what their rabbi had told them about their recent ordeal together, so there was already a respect for his quiet persistence in pursuing a goal that had the potential for great good for so many people.

After the service, as Joshua and his mother walked out, people were very gracious to them, congratulating Miriam not only for her beauty, but also for having a son who was so dedicated to helping others. They felt proud that they both had worshipped at their synagogue.

As the crowd thinned out, Joshua and Miriam walked up the street, chatting casually as they walked along.

"Son, they are such nice people. It was good to be with our own again, after so long a time. Didn't you feel at home, too?"

"Yes, Mother, our people haven't changed much over the years. I am so glad you could spend those few minutes with them. I could tell they loved you immediately. It showed in their warm looks as they talked to you."

"I am proud, Joshua, that they accepted you as one of them. You could have a much different effect on them today than in other times. These people are more open to the truth you came to bring them. If you spent more time with them, I know you could win their hearts."

"I can see that, Mother, but that is not to be. They must see my goodness in the purity and integrity of the lives of my followers. If those who called themselves Christians followed my ways, the Jewish people could see that I still live. But instead my followers have hurt our people cruelly through the centuries, so it is too humiliating for them to accept my message now. However, they follow my ways without even realizing it. In our old days, they were obsessed with the observance of law as a sure way to salvation. Now they are well-known for their concern for humanity, as I always taught. Many now believe in heaven, which was not true when I promised it to my disciples back then. It is the Christians who have gone back to the rigid observance of law to find salvation, and so many of those obsessed with law are notorious for their lack of compassion. I still love our people. There is so much goodness in them. They are always eager to learn."

Joshua was aware that they were being followed. His mother realized it as well.

"Son, I guess you know we are being followed. Does it bother you?"

"Mother, is it any different from before? No, it does not bother me in the least. In fact, I am enjoying it this time. I play this game with them. What they don't know is that my surveillance system is far more advanced than theirs. I know their every move even before they make it. At the right time, I make my move and it throws their plans into disarray. It exasperates them because they can't understand what went wrong. They mean well, Mother, because they think they are protecting the country, like overly religious people fear those who promote needed change. Rather than talk with them, they label them the enemy. They damage many people's lives by their unreasonable suspicion. They see evil and danger in the most innocent of people.

"Mother, I appreciate your helping the people who have been so troubled of late. You might like to visit some of their families to comfort them."

"I will do that, Joshua. I have already visited some Muslim families. They were shocked at first, but the women understood who I was, and they were surprised when I told them that you sent me. But they were very pleased. This surely is different from the way we ordinarily enter people's lives. The Muslims particularly are shocked, but they were comforted. I know it touches their hearts to know that you care for them, my son."

As the two strolled through the neighborhood, the surveillance van was never far behind, always, so the agents thought, at a discreetly unnoticeable distance. At one point, however, as

Joshua and his mother turned a corner, Joshua continued walking, but Miriam was no longer at his side. The agents, thinking she had entered the corner house, called their office and insisted they establish a surveillance of that house.

Knowing what was happening, Joshua just smiled.

SINCE THE MEETING AT IBRAHIM'S HOUSE, THINGS STARTED moving fast. Ibrahim was not a man to waste time. He had an intensive meeting with Elie and gave him detailed instructions on what he expected of him. He gave him a list of names and addresses of key people in the Middle East and told him never to put them to paper. He had to memorize them all, which was not the slightest problem for the young man, as he had a prodigious memory, if not photographic, then "audiographic"—whatever he heard he remembered.

At the airport, Elie was searched in every way. His name alone made him suspect. His whereabouts had been monitored ever since the detainment of all Joshua's friends. He had been followed to the airport, and agents in Jordan were alerted about him so his every movement there could be tracked. The ride over was routine. He had traveled this and other routes to Europe and the Middle East many times. The only difference this time was a friendship he struck up with one of the flight attendants, Anna Maria, who was the daughter of one of Elie's dear friends. Their conversation made the ten-hour flight seem considerably shorter.

Elie was overwhelmed at the welcome he received at the airport in Amman. He knew Ibrahim had business connections around the world, but he never dreamed of the reception that awaited him as he entered the terminal. Thinking that no one there would even know him, much less expect his arrival, he was shocked to find a group of people waiting. Two men were holding a four-foot banner that read in Arabic, "Welcome, Mr. Zambaka!" Elie immediately broke out into a broad smile, showing his sparkling white teeth.

Everyone took their turn with effusive Arabic hugs and kisses, each person telling his or her name—which, to everyone's stunned surprise later on, Elie remembered. Once he'd exited the terminal, Elie was whisked away to a massive villa on a hill outside the city. It was a breathtaking sight, both the view of the surrounding valley spread out before one's eyes and the majesty of the architectural design of the house itself. The house was framed in real cedar trees, tall, thin junipers, and Lombardy poplars. Magnificent gardens were watered from a deep well. The place was owned by a dear friend of Ibrahim's named Ibn Saud, a man of great proportions in many ways, including an expansive jovial disposition. He took to Elie immediately, and the friendship grew with each day.

Ibn was proud of his gardens, terraced and manicured with artistic precision. His first concern was whether or not his guest had been able to sleep on the plane. If not, then he should take a nap before they began the day. It was almost noon already. If he did not need a rest, then they could jump right into the day. Fortunately, Elie could sleep anywhere and at any time, so he assured his host that he was wide awake and curious to see everything.

"Well, in that case, friend, let me show you my gardens. As you can see, they are all over the estate, and each one is different, with different plants and shrubs and trees."

After pouring tea, which had been brewing, the two began their journey around the estate. The whole tour took well over an hour. The formal gardens were spectacular. The flowers were organized in such a way that there was always color. When one variety of plant passed its bloom time, other varieties took its place. Many of the plants were perennials, some were biennials, and the rest changed each year. Elie was particularly impressed with the rose garden. There were over two thousand bushes that covered the better part of an acre, with paths winding their way through the whole area. Marble garden benches were placed strategically along the paths so tired visitors could rest before they went on with their walk. In the garden were roses Elie had never seen before, and he remarked at how impressed he was not only with the beauty of the garden itself, but also with the uniqueness of some of the blooms and their vast variety and exotic colors.

"Thank you, Elie, they are my favorites. I love my roses. I cultivate that garden myself and have produced my own hybrids, so you will see here varieties you will not see anywhere else. I am so glad you like them."

"Mr. Saud, may I ask where you ever found a gardener to create such a landscaping masterpiece?" Elie asked him.

"Some I brought in from Italy, and others came from Japan. At first I was worried they might not work well together, but after a few weeks they became best of friends, helping each other every chance they get. In fact, it is comical hearing the Italians trying to speak Japanese and the Japanese trying to speak Italian. But it is an experience listening to them, as both nationalities are excitable, and when they are happy or upset about something, I can hear them all the way up to the house."

"They are remarkable artists," Elie commented. "I have never seen such beautiful gardens."

"Thank you. I am quite proud of them. Let me show you a very special garden. It is isolated and closed off by a labyrinth of tall hedges."

As the two men walked through the labyrinth, they eventually came to a shrine, with the most impressive garden leading up to it. Immediately in front of the shrine were four marble benches specially sculpted so one could sit for a long time and not be uncomfortable. The center of the shrine was an inspiring likeness of a shepherd taking a helpless lamb from a patch of briars.

The two men stood motionless for a long time, each wrapped in his own thoughts. Finally, Elie broke the silence. "Is that a statue of who I think it is?"

"This is my private chapel, or perhaps mosque, I should call it, as I am a Muslim. But in my heart, Jesus is my dearest friend, and I accept him as my Savior. I come here daily and often spend hours contemplating the beauty of his life and his teachings. His teachings are so far superior to those of any other way of life, but few people take him seriously anymore. If we all listened to him, we would not have this terrible hatred in the world today. Accepting his teaching on forgiveness is the key to peace in this world, but people would rather hate and punish than forgive, so our world goes up in flames. I used the figure of the Good Shepherd so visitors will think it is just a statue of a gentle, caring shepherd. But it is my shrine to Jesus. I know you are a Catholic and would appreciate this little chapel."

"I am deeply moved, Mr. Saud. I could spend hours here

myself, alone with the Good Shepherd, whom I need to heal me of all the inner turmoil that troubles me day and night."

"Dear friend, you are welcome to come here anytime you like, and I guarantee you will never be disturbed while you are here in meditation."

"Thank you, thank you so much. I would like to do that sometime."

"Well, are you tired yet after your long plane ride and our long trip through the gardens?" Ibn asked him.

"No. I am a little tired, though in a strange way refreshed. But I could use a brief siesta."

"I'll bring you to your room, and you can wash up and rest as long as you like. When you come back down, we will have our meal, so don't feel you have to follow a tight schedule. Tomorrow will be busy enough. Today, just rest. Also, I made arrangements for your flight to Tehran. You said you needed a brief stay there to make a few contacts. It is only for an overnight. Am I correct?"

"Thank you so much for you thoughtfulness. I know now I need a rest," Elie told his host.

There was no shortcut through the garden. It took a full twenty minutes to reach the entrance to the gardens and then return to the house. Elie was tired indeed as his mind reeled from all the thoughts that absorbed him in his meditation at the shrine. His whole life passed before him in those few minutes, and it was almost as if God were preparing him for the future and all that was about to happen.

It was seven o'clock when Elie woke up. It was a perfect place to sleep, as there was no noise except for the singing of the birds in the trees outside his bedroom window. After taking a shower and dressing, he went downstairs and apologized to Ibn Saud for being so late.

"Late! No one is late around here. Supper is prepared and we eat when everyone is ready. So you are right on time. Did you sleep well?"

"The best sleep I ever had. I can't tell you how good I feel," Elie responded.

As the two were talking, the rest of the family started to gather for supper. Entering the dining room, Elie was shocked by the size of the formal table. Nothing small about anything in this place! The table could easily seat twenty people, and in a few minutes, every seat was taken. Elie was seated at the right hand of his host and felt quite honored.

When everyone was seated, Mr. Saud stood up and introduced his guest to everyone: his wife, Naomi, who sat at her husband's left, then his six children, four boys and two girls, all grown and in their twenties. Farther down the table were cousins and other relatives, and at the far end were the Japanese and Sicilian gardeners. Again, Elie remembered each of their names, and afterward, when everyone gathered in a large drawing room for Turkish delights and Arabic coffee, they were all surprised when he called each of them by name. He had the most fun, however, with the Japanese and Sicilian gardeners and a visiting Polish gardener on vacation by the name of Dave Bogatka. Together they were a lively bunch, and Elie thoroughly enjoyed their happy banter, especially that of the Polish gardener, who expressed a number of unorthodox landscaping techniques.

"I am glad you're enjoying yourself, Elie," Mr. Saud said as he approached the little group. "I enjoy these men myself. They're not only good workers, they are also the life of the villa. I should put them on television." The men just smiled. Very sensitive to protocol, they spoke to their boss only when he spoke to them.

"Elie, we have a long day tomorrow, so I'll be retiring soon. I'll be down for breakfast at seven. But feel free to sleep a little longer if you need it. Have you ever been to Aqaba or Petra?"

"I went to Aqaba many years ago with my family. I grew up in Iran and traveled extensively with my family. I have never been to Petra."

"Good, we can take a trip down there. I think you'll enjoy it. I would not be surprised if the three Wise Men who visited the infant Jesus stopped there on the way to Bethlehem to purchase their gifts of frankincense and myrrh. That was the great center of trade in those days for all kinds of exotic and precious gifts."

Soon the little party dissolved; the fun and laughter settled into a whisper, and then an almost monastic silence, as everyone retired for the evening. Looking forward to a good night's sleep, Elie was glad to go to his room, where a cool breeze floated gently through the window and across his room. He was asleep by the time he reached his last prayer. Though he had survived the long plane ride, it was a long day and the time difference took its toll. Fortunately, the ancient stone walls were almost a foot and a half thick; otherwise the whole villa would have been victim to Elie's horrific snoring.

II

To everyone's surprise, Elie was the first to rise the next morning, or so he thought. It was a perfect day, cool, brilliantly clear, the kind of day when one would enjoy sightseeing. But that was not on Elie's mind. As soon as he showered, shaved, and dressed, he hurried down to the garden and managed, after running into a few dead ends, to find the shrine of the Good Shepherd.

To his surprise, someone else had beaten him there. Sitting on a bench, absorbed in prayer, was his host. Elie thought he would spend a few quiet minutes there alone, talking to the Savior. He wondered how many hours Ibn Saud had been sitting there. Though he was a jovial man, he was like an artesian well, bubbly on the surface, but with springs so deep that few could plumb the depths. Elie could sense that his host was a man of intense feeling, one concerned about the troubles brewing all around him. He was concerned for his family, and even for those who depended on him, like his Japanese and Sicilian gardeners. It was his trust in the Good Shepherd that gave him peace and a serenity that gave him strength.

Elie, too, had gone down to that shrine for peace and serenity. Much like Ibn Saud, Elie could be bubbly on the surface, but his thoughts and concerns ran deep beneath the surface. He was a person difficult to reach even by those who loved him most, the kind who suffered pain alone but was always there to help others in pain. Knowing him, one could understand how he could feel the loneliness and pain of each homeless person he met on the street. Now he was in pain himself, a pain he could not define, the pain of anxiety and fear of the future, a future that was unforeseeable and unknown. No one could help him. No one could understand his apprehension, not only because there was no one with whom he could share his mission, but also because there was no one who could see the future in such detail as to know the danger that caused him such frightful premonitions.

So now he fell on his knees far behind Ibn Saud so as not to distract him and sat back on his heels, placing his folded hands in his lap. He looked up at the statue, then lowered his head and was soon lost in thought, prayer, or profound contemplation, whatever it was; he stayed there motionless for the next half hour and was unaware even when Ibn Saud finished his own prayer and walked past him on his way back to the house.

When he finally did come back to life, he was surprised to find his host gone and more surprised when he looked at his watch and realized the time. Knowing his host wanted to get an early start while it was still cool, he ran through the labyrinth and, after three times around, finally found the exit. Ibn Saud was watching him and laughing as he called his family to watch the spectacle from the kitchen window.

When Elie at last exited the maze, perspiring profusely, the whole family was on the patio, cheering him on and clapping loudly, much to his embarrassment. Once he was on the patio, they all hugged him and assured him that he wasn't late; in fact, they had a rule that nothing on the schedule started until everyone arrived, especially for breakfast. And for that they all took turns being late, except for Ibn Saud, who disappeared every morning before anyone else even thought of getting out of bed. Ibn guffawed at realizing for the first time that his family noticed his early morning disappearances.

A Westerner could hardly have called the family's breakfast a feast, because goat cheese and fish and figs and oranges and pita bread were not ordinary Western fare. But Elie's older relatives ate like that, so the meal brought back many childhood memories.

"Well, young man, would you like to offer thanks to God?" his host asked Elie.

"If you like, but we always reserved that honor for the head of the family," Elie replied respectfully.

"Thank you," Ibn said with a gracious smile at Elie's delicate sense of respect for his host.

"Father in heaven, we have much to be grateful for. You have been so generous and merciful toward all of us. We are particularly grateful this day because You have sent to us a remarkable young man who shares with us values we hold sacred, a man who is willing to lay down his life as Jesus did to save his fellow human beings who are suffering so much in this frightfully tormented world. Father, bless us all this day as we are about to begin our appointed tasks. May we do them well for Your honor and glory, and always be aware of Your presence with us. Bless our guest and make fruitful the dangerous task You have called him to undertake. Be by his side each moment to guide his steps and give him strength. Finally, Father, bless this food for which we thank You, being always mindful that there are many who will go hungry today. Praise be Allah!"

To which everyone responded a hearty "Amen."

"I like that prayer, Ibn, it is very thoughtful. It reminded me of a saying attributed to Jesus in the writings of one of your holy men, which describes so poetically the plight of the poor as God sees them: 'Hunger is my seasoning, fear is my garment, wool is my clothing, the light of the dawn is my heat in winter, the moon is my lantern, my legs are my beast of burden, and the produce of the earth is my food and fruit. I retire for the night with nothing to my name; I wake in the morning with nothing to my name. And there is no one on earth who is richer than I.'"

"Elie, that is very touching," Ibn replied. "Yes, our holy men of the past had many quotes of Jesus' sayings. Where they came from, I don't know, but many of them are similar to his sayings in the Gospels."

Elie and Mr. Saud started late on their outing. The sun was already high and the air was hot, but the air-conditioned Mercedes assured a pleasant ride. The first stop was not far from Amman, a place called Madaba, an ancient city famous for a large mosaic map made of millions of tiny colored ceramic chips. It was a map of old Palestine, showing the Dead Sea, the Nile River, Jerusalem, and the Church of the Holy Sepulcher, which was already finished by the time the mosaic was made in the sixth century. Other fascinating sites were an exciting adventure for Elie, even though he and his family had traveled extensively. These sites he and his family had missed completely.

The trip from Madaba to Petra took close to an hour. Petra is an ancient city, full of some of the most fascinating objects and pieces of architecture in the world. Elie was awestruck at the sight of the city carved in the face of a cliff. It is breathtaking, and much of the detail is in excellent condition. Petra was once the capital of the Nabataeans, ancient people who flourished for centuries before Jesus and for many years afterward. The place fell into ruins later on and was discovered again just a hundred or so years ago. Elie was convinced that Ibn was right: the Magi who visited Jesus stopped there on their way from Persia to purchase gifts for the family of the newborn King, as Petra was a famous trading center in the old days.

There were so many things to see in Petra, Ibn decided they should stay another day. It was too late for them to visit the ancient monastery or the huge Roman amphitheater. Also, the view from the top of the cliffs was an experience Ibn did not want Elie to miss. So they found a hotel and stayed for another day, then returned home. Elie talked the whole rest of the trip about the many things that he had never heard of before and how deeply impressed he was, particularly at how wonderfully preserved all the ancient sites were.

Their touring on the next day was more relaxed, and they enjoyed the remarkable and curious details of this ancient wonder.

When they arrived home late that afternoon, Elie was not only tired, but famished. The food on their trip was not to his liking, so he ate little. Now he could eat a camel, he was so hungry.

"We have some time before supper, Elie," Ibn told his guest. "I'm going to rest a little. Take your time. You might also want to take a nap. We'll be eating in about an hour, so just make yourself at home."

The whole evening, including dinnertime, was spent with the two men sharing their experiences with the rest of the family. Of course, everyone there had been to Petra, but everyone's experiences are different, and they could see just how different

Elie's experiences were from theirs. Ibn Saud was surprised at how much Elie had absorbed of all he had seen the last two days.

"Elie, you are amazing," Ibn commented. "I cannot get over what a prodigious memory you have. You tell the stories about everything we've seen the past two days with such detail, you would put even a tour guide to shame."

Elie wasn't conscious of his prodigious memory, though it was a security asset when remembering minute details of critical situations that could be life-threatening. But the most important thing on his mind at this point was his empty stomach. What he craved most was something juicy, like fruit. Elie never ate as much fruit as he did that night: at least four oranges, three bananas, and a handful of dates, together with his Arabic coffee.

"I have not had so much fun in years, Mr. Saud," Elie said by way of thanking his host for the wonderful time they had spent together, as well as the exquisite meals they have been eating since he arrived. "You have all been so kind and so gracious. I will never forget you and will pray for you always."

The day ended well, and Elie felt misgivings about starting out on his mission the next day. His overnight trip to Tehran would be brief enough, but he was uneasy about discussing with people there the purpose of his mission. The Iranians were not Arabs; they were Persians. They had little sympathy for Palestinians. The only possible benefit accruing from a peace deal would be the opening of trade with Israel and a possible warming of relations with the United States. The reality of what he had agreed to do was beginning to hit him, but there was no turning back. He had committed himself to trying to do what seemed impossible: establish contact with key Iranian businessmen, Palestinian leaders, and terrorists, as well as powerful Israelis, in an attempt to speak sense to them and hope they would see the reasonableness of his proposal. And it was not his proposal. It was the well-considered judgment of all the rational members of Ibrahim's and Joshua's friends. Ibrahim's name alone carried great weight in the Middle East. Elie was hoping Ibrahim's reputation and the high esteem in which he was held would lend credibility to the messages he was bringing.

His sleep that night was fitful. He kept waking, wondering where he was and what might be happening that day. Finally, unable to sleep, he tried to pray. Curiously, the image of Joshua kept coming before his mind, and he found himself praying to Joshua. For some reason, he had an entirely new image of Joshua and who he might be, so he felt quite comfortable praying to him. This made him feel strangely secure in the realization that his mission could not fail. After all, it was Joshua's personal project, and if God was for it, how could it fail? Success of the mission, however, did not necessarily guarantee the survival of the messenger. But then he had the assurance he was doing God's work, and that gave him strength no matter what might happen to him.

He awoke early the next morning and went out into the garden, through the maze, and to the shrine of the Good Shepherd, where he underwent a profound mystical experience: He knew God was there. It wasn't until after he finished his meditation that he noticed Ibn sitting off to the corner. Elie had the feeling that his friend was carrying a heavy weight. He could sense it in the way he prayed with such intensity, as if he desperately needed God to come to his aid. Not that there were any body movements or prayerful gestures. In fact, Ibn was motionless, but Elie's own pain made him aware of pain in those close to him. Ordinarily, he would distance himself so he would not have to feel their pain constantly. His own pain was enough for him to bear, sometimes even too much. His first impulse now was to approach his host and ask if he was going through something he might like to share, but then he thought he might be intruding on Ibn's privacy, and that would be rude.

At that moment, as if Ibn Saud sensed Elie's presence, he turned and saw Elie watching him.

"Elie, I noticed you deep in prayer before and was tempted to wish you a good morning, but I did not want to disturb you."

"I could not help but notice you praying so intensely. Are you hurting, my friend?" Elie asked his host.

"Elie, I rarely share my life with anyone, but, yes, I am deeply troubled. Life is so horribly complicated here. Everyone thinks I have it all together, but inside I am in turmoil. It is all so complicated. I am a Muslim, but I know that Jesus is really the Son of God and will one day be my judge. I built this shrine to surreptitiously spend time praying to him without anyone realizing what I am really doing. But what do I do in a totally Islamic country where one is not free to follow his conscience, but must live and worship the way everyone else demands he worship? I feel I am being destroyed."

"You are a good man, Ibn. Do you not think that God understands? Your whole life reflects Jesus' goodness, and every morning I see you here deep in contemplation. That is more than most Christians do."

"Perhaps, but I want so much to be able to go to church and take part in the worship service of Christians, so I can really feel I have made a commitment to the Lord. And more than anything else, I want to be able to receive the Eucharist. My grandmother baptized me when I was an infant and secretly told me about Jesus. Now I have this burning desire to share my life with him and to do his work."

"Dear friend, you are doing his work. When you get a chance, stop into a church and receive the Eucharist. I am sure the priest will understand. Over here they are different. They are more sensitive to the people's predicaments."

"Do you think that would be acceptable?"

"Look at Nicodemus! He came to Jesus in the middle of the night because he was afraid someone would report him if he went to visit with him during the day. Jesus accepted his good-will, and honest intentions, and understood his fears."

"Elie, thank you. I feel better already. But I have to tell you, it was not just about myself I was praying. I was also praying for you. I am worried about the mission you are undertaking. It will be very difficult, and very few people would have the sagacity and inner tranquillity to even think of embarking on such a project. But you are a very special person, and I know God will be with you every step of the way. And you will be in my prayers every day. I also would appreciate it very much if you would pray for me and my family. Times here are frightening, and life is not easy."

"You have my assurance of that, my friend. I will never forget you or what you have done for me."

"Elie, after breakfast I would like to chat with you on the way to the airport. I have the names that our friend Ibrahim asked me to give you. Three of them are in Tehran. I have already contacted them, so they will be expecting you. They promised to use whatever influence they have to make your mission a success. They cannot believe that an American would put his life at such risk for a purpose that is really not an American problem. They can't wait to meet you and welcome you."

"Thank you, Ibn. I feel more at peace now that you told me this. I have to admit I am worried, and terribly frightened. But I know God is with me."

"Let us go up to breakfast. Everyone is going to be wondering where we are."

Elie's flight to Iran was uneventful. He met with some old friends, and made contact with those to whom he was to deliver messages, and had dinner with his friends, and on the next morning returned to Amman, where Ibn Saud met him at the airport.

"How did it go, Elie?"

"Very well. I could not share much with the people I met. They were most gracious to me, and our brief conversations were to the point. They listened but did not in any way commit themselves. This is why I was not to stay there long. What we discussed will fall into place if the rest of my mission is successful. The Persians are fundamentally businesspeople. They are not going to miss an opportunity to enter into lucrative contracts. So we shall see."

Elie stayed with Ibn Saud and his family for a few more days. He felt very much at home with these wonderful people. When the time finally came for him to continue on his mission, it was a sad occasion. Breakfast that morning was a warm, emotional gathering. Everyone had grown to love Elie, and he them. They wished he could spend more time, but that was not to be.

After breakfast, Ibn Saud gave detailed instructions to Elie, who needed no notes or pages of names and addresses. He remembered everything. Written instructions and directions, however, he did need to make sure he would find the places and the people he needed to contact. As his host read off the names, Elie was impressed with the important people he knew on a personal basis, key people in Lebanon, commanders in the Hezbollah, their contacts in the Syrian government and military, war lords in Lebanon, both Muslim and Christian, moderate and radical politicians in Iran. These were the people Elie was expected to convince of the need for peace in the area. He was beginning to realize the immensity of the responsibility Ibrahim had placed upon him, and he wondered if his friend was just a dreamer who had no practical ability to carry through in a way that made sense. Did he really think that he could talk these men so full of hatred into seeing the value of making peace with those they had been taught to hate since childhood, convince them to use their influence to persuade others to embrace their enemies? Yet that is what Jesus taught. Could one say that Jesus lacked common sense? Hardly. If anyone knew human nature, it was Jesus. He designed it. Maybe Ibrahim was just the one rare person who took his faith in Jesus seriously enough to believe that Jesus' teachings could work, especially his teaching about forgiveness, which most Christians ignored as naïve and out of touch with reality. Maybe the world was in the mess it was in because people would not take Jesus seriously and give to the world his example of how to live as God's children, and as brothers and sisters, treating others with mercy and forgiveness.

"Elie," his host called out to him, "are you all right? You look as if you are a thousand miles away."

"I am just overwhelmed with the number of important people you know and, I must say, the types of people. Doesn't life get terribly complicated for you?"

"It does, but I have many things I want to accomplish, and it is important for me to know the good and the bad. It is a difficult juggling act, but I maintain my integrity, so I am respected by both kinds, and they trust me, because they know I am not scheming for myself."

"Still, it is dangerous."

"Yes, as you are about to find out. You now have all the information you need. I am giving you a car to use on your way, so you don't have to depend on anyone else for transportation. The car has a built-in satellite telephone, so you can call anywhere with it. Don't worry about the bill. You might want to call your family to keep them from worrying. But be discreet and brief, and if you call home, call from an out-of-the-way place. Call me anytime you need, either here at the house or on my satellite phone. Please be careful! You may not fully realize how perilous this mission is. These people are complicated and devious and trust no one whom they haven't known for a long time. You will be a stranger to them, and it is only their respect for Ibrahim and me that will permit them to talk with you. Even so, they will watch your every move and try to monitor your phone calls. So be prudent, and weigh your words. Don't say anything to anyone that you would not say in the presence of persons on the opposite side."

After giving him directions to Damascus, he had one of the servants put in the car an insulated container full of food and beverages, so he could better enjoy his long trip. Ibn's family came down to the driveway to wish Elie well and promised their prayers. Ibn expressed the feelings of the whole family: "Elie, though you have been here for only a few days, you have become a member of our family and a true soul brother to me. I will pray for you many times every day."

With tears in his eyes, Elie hugged his friend. "And you

have become a brother to me, the brother I never had. There is no way I can thank you for your goodness and your generosity. I hope this mission will succeed."

"God be with you, Elie."

"And with you, my friend."

I T WAS A LONELY RIDE FROM AMMAN TO DAMASCUS. IBN
Saud's family were warm and accepting, and it was difficult
going off into a dangerous unknown after being lavished with
so much affection. The desert surrounding Elie mirrored his
mood, dry, empty, and without life. The feeling of loneliness
frightened him. He might as well be on a planet out in space.
He had never felt so alone. Was it a premonition of some impending disaster? Was it the devil trying to frighten him into
abandoning his mission? He knew he could not give up. What
he was about to do was too important. He knew in his heart it
was the work of God, so different from politicians trying to
broker a peace deal. With them it was just a deal in which even
the broker had his angle. Elie knew in his heart his undertaking
could make a difference, even if the results were not immediately evident. At least he was planting the seeds that would
slowly germinate and eventually take root. He might never live
to see it—a possibility that was beginning to preoccupy his

thoughts more frequently as he moved each moment closer to the center of hell. He missed his family terribly. It might be a good time to call them. Ibn Saud had told him to use the phone to call his family, and he was in the middle of nowhere, ten miles from Mafrak and seventy miles from Damascus.

How fascinating to be using satellite signals to call home, Elie thought as he dialed his sister's number.

In just a few seconds, he heard the phone ringing. His heart pounded with excitement, then he heard his sister's voice. "Hello."

"Joan, it's me."

"Elie, where are you?"

"On vacation in Syria, checking out sites to send my customers for vacation."

"Are you okay?"

"Yes, I am wonderful. Just spent time with some extraordinary people. In fact, they gave me their car to use for my trip. I feel like a big shot in the diplomatic corps. I guess that's what I really am."

"What do you mean? Now you got me worried. What are you doing over there?"

"I'm really on business. I was given excellent contacts and all kinds of introductions. I can't wait to meet some of these people. You'd be proud of me."

"Elie, you're crazy. What a time to go to those places to find vacation spots for your clients!"

"Don't worry about me. I'm having a great time. Where is Richard?"

"He's not here. But little Richard is."

"Good. Would you put him on? Then I'll have to go."

"Hello, Uncle Elie. I miss you."

"I miss you, too, Richard. Aren't you working today?"

"No, I have off today, so I'm helping my mother. When are you coming home?"

"Soon, I hope. As soon as I get my work done here. Pray for me, Richard. I know God always listens to your prayers. Tell everybody I love them, and I love you, too. Good-bye for now."

Elie rubbed his eyes to clear his vision. His memories of home made the time pass more quickly, and he soon found himself at the border. He had no trouble crossing the border, especially after the border guard read the introductory letter from Ibn Saud, who had previously alerted the officer in charge of the post. It was not a big city, but Elie was surprised to see Arabs of all descriptions. Some he could identify as Chechens, and when he stopped to get gas, the attendants were Palestinians. In an hour and a half, he would be in Damascus. He had been there several times before as a young boy with his parents, and though there were many memories, he had no feelings of nostalgia for the ancient Oriental bazaars or Islamic monuments.

On his arrival, he drove past some of those old childhood memories. Damascus was an ancient city, going back perhaps five thousand years. Ruins were strewn over every part of the city, testifying to the many cultures that at one time thrived there. But Elie was a man with a purpose and wanted only to throw himself into his mission. His coming had been anticipated, and when Ibn Saud's car was spotted, the information was phoned to President Assad's secretary's office. Instructions were given to escort the car to the home of Tariq Hassan, the president's confidant and a person on whose counsel President Assad strongly depended.

A column of palm trees lined the road leading up to Hassan's home. The house itself was a gleaming white structure with a red tile roof and bars on all the windows. Unlike Ibn Saud's house, this estate reflected the owner's highly disciplined personality. Hassan was a man of few personal needs and an almost monastic austerity. In fact, he had once intended to become a monk but left before his final vows.

On his arrival, Elie was met at the entrance by two of the servants; one took charge of his luggage as the other ushered him into an austerely appointed waiting room.

"Mr. Hassan has been eagerly awaiting your coming," the servant said respectfully. "Mr. Saud has already told him all about you, so Mr. Hassan looks forward to welcoming you as a friend. My name is Tarif Khalil. Should you need anything during your stay here, just call for me. The other gentleman has already brought your luggage to your room."

"Thank you, Tarif," Elie replied in Arabic as the servant withdrew.

It was not long before Mr. Hassan entered the room. Elie stood to meet him.

"Peace be with you, Mr. Zambaka."

"And with you peace, Mr. Hassan."

Soon the two men drifted from English to Arabic. Elie could tell his host was much more relaxed speaking in his native tongue, so he graciously initiated the shift, which delighted Mr. Hassan.

"You come here with a most flattering introduction by our dear friend Mr. Saud," Mr. Hassan commented. "He and I have been friends for many years, and it is a friendship I value most highly. He has already briefed me on the purpose of your journey, but that can wait until another time. Right now you must be hungry. The trip from Amman is not the most comfortable. Would you like to rest first, or should we have a light lunch?"

"A light lunch would be most welcome," Elie replied.

Mr. Hassan rang for one of the servants and told him to have the cook prepare lunch for the two of them.

Even the dining room was austere. A long table simply carved and made locally was surrounded by twelve chairs of the same design. On the wall above a buffet was an oil painting of a monastery, the monastery of so many sacred memories for Mr. Hassan.

As the two men sat, the cook brought out platters of various cheeses and fruit and pita bread and a large pot of tea.

"Is this the first time you have visited our country?" the official asked Elie.

"No, I came here many times when I was a boy. My father was a businessman and often took me with him. However, your rulers have made many changes, and the city is much more beautiful than it was when I was a boy."

"Yes, we have worked hard in spite of very difficult conditions in this part of the world. Our mutual friend Mr. Abboud helped us immensely with his generous contributions for the construction of one of our colleges. He is a remarkable man. I am aware that he has arranged for you to visit us. How is he? He was not feeling well the last time he was here. He works very hard, and I think sometimes, in spite of his great energy, he pushes himself beyond the limits. I hope he takes time to rest."

"You must have given him that advice, because he now takes a rest in the afternoon, if he does not have unexpected appointments," Elie assured him.

"Mr. Zambaka, our friend called and informed me of your coming to visit us. I have to admit I was stunned by his proposal. On first flush it seemed totally unrealistic and doomed to failure from the start. But Ibrahim is not an empty-headed dreamer. He is most practical and possessed of much common sense. I have been pondering our conversation ever since, and I am beginning to realize this horrible mess between Israel and the Palestinians has to be resolved for the benefit of us all. The prosperity of all our countries has been put on hold because of this chaotic conflict. Maybe this is the time, with God's help, and with all of us working together, when we can bring about a happy resolution to this conflict. But we can talk about that after you rest. I will show you to your room."

Elie rested for a solid two hours, then wandered back downstairs, where he encountered one of the servants.

"How was your rest?" the man asked in very broken English.

When Elie replied in Arabic, the man was surprised and continued speaking to him in his own tongue.

"I hope you enjoy your stay here, sir. I will show you around the house so you will know where you are going." This the man did, and in the process, he described the history of the villa, which dated back four hundred years. After conducting Elie on a grand tour, he led him to the garden in the rear of the house and left him there to enjoy the peace and quiet of the simple but colorful plot of neatly arranged shrubs and flower beds.

Left with his thoughts, Elie wandered along the paths, enjoying the fragrance of the flowers and the freedom of the butterflies as they moved from one blossom to another, so happy, so carefree. Still tired from his journey, he sat on one of the chairs in the shade and soon drifted off into a deep sleep. His thoughts wandered from his childhood in Iran, to the happy times of his early boyhood, to the difficulties of later years. In the middle of his dreams, the easy flow of memories was interrupted by a presence that seemed all too real. He dreamed of Joshua, and it was as if he were standing there in front of him, assuring him not to be afraid and telling him just what he must say to the people he would be visiting. "Listen to what they have to say to you, because they will have their own reasons for feeling differently. So don't discount the validity of their feelings and their reasoning. Be patient, and gently remind them that unless someone has the wisdom and the courage to break the chain of hatred, it will continue to wreak havoc and eventually will destroy their own children and grandchildren. Their place in history and their own eternal destiny depends upon the choice they make."

When Elie woke a few minutes later, he was surprised that Joshua was not there. He felt a strange feeling of loneliness, but also a feeling that he was not alone, that in some way Joshua was nearby, assuring him that he need not be afraid of all the uncertainties facing him. It was God's work he was doing, and God would protect him and guide him along the way.

A servant appeared, spied him on his chair, and hurried over. "Oh, Mr. Zambaka, here you are. Mr. Secretary Hassan asked if you would be interested in a short trip to the Old City. He is in his office. I will bring you there, if you will follow me."

"Thank you. I have not seen the Old City since I was a boy. I got lost there one day and my mother almost went crazy looking for me."

"Mr. Zambaka, how was your rest in the garden?" Mr. Hassan asked as Elie entered his office. "I love to go out there just to think and daydream about what life could be like. It gives me strength."

"I had a marvelous time. After admiring all your beautiful flowers and shrub arrangements, I sat down and drifted into another world. Now I feel fully refreshed. And, yes, I would like very much to visit the Old City again."

"Good, I will be ready in five minutes, and we can drive down. It takes only a few minutes to get there."

Damascus is Syria's largest city and also its capital. Originally, it was an oasis that drew people from all over the surrounding desert; the nearby river made it possible for the population to swell eventually into a city. A main attraction today is the Old City, with its ancient Roman wall, the wall over which St. Paul was let down during the night for his escape from his enemies.

On the way to the Old City, Tariq Hassan grilled Elie, not in a belligerent way, but in an attempt to learn the details of his approach to all these mutually hostile people he was scheduled to meet.

"Elie, if I may presume to call you by your first name—and please call me by my baptismal name, as I am proud of it—Elie, what you are attempting to undertake seems, on the surface, to be an impossible dream. I won't say it is doomed to failure, but greater men than you and I have attempted to do something similar and were met with abuse and rejection. If our friend Ibrahim was not an instigator of this dream, I would be inclined to refuse to become involved, but he is such a practical, hard-nosed businessman, I am sure he must see some value in it that eludes me completely."

"Tariq, for you to understand, it would be necessary for you to have been with us from the beginning. It was not Ibrahim who began this undertaking. There was a man, a Jew, a rather strange man, who just became a part of all of our lives. Some of us are Christians, some are Muslims, some are Jews. The man is fearless and possesses a confidence the likes of which I have never seen. And yet he is not arrogant, but has a very humble bearing and treats everyone with respect. It is his dream. He has already been arrested by the government agents, but he was not in the slightest ruffled over it. In fact, he made a remarkable comment one day, which I never forgot. He said he had a much more efficient surveillance system than the agents and so could always keep ahead of what they were planning. Life for him reminds me of a chess game, which he seems to know he cannot lose. His confidence spilled over to all of us. That is why we are so willing to be part of this mission. We all call it a mission, because we are convinced that it is what God is trying to accomplish through us."

"Elie, I'm trying not to be impressed, but what you say is very touching. What is this man's name?"

"Joshua, Joshua ben-Youssef."

"Elie, have you given thought to the meaning of that name?"

"Not particularly."

"Joshua in our language means Jesus. And ben-Youssef means son of Joseph. Jesus, son of Joseph. Doesn't that chill you? Is he just an ordinary man?"

"I never considered it that way. That gives me goose bumps to think of it. Do you think . . . ?"

"I have no idea. I cannot imagine in this day and age something like that happening, but who knows the mind of God. God uses instruments, human instruments, to accomplish His dreams. He does not act on His own. Maybe Ibrahim knows something we do not know, and perhaps that is what makes him so confident. Ibrahim is a very spiritual man, I would even say a saintly man. He certainly could sense the hand of God in something before it would even dawn on anyone else. What precisely do you propose that we here in Syria can do?"

"The Hezbollah," Elie started to say.

"Yes, I know, I know. That is going to be a gigantic obstacle. Those people are imports from Iran, and they are mostly in Lebanon. It is difficult not to support them without being considered an enemy of their movement. They are fanatic followers of the dead Ayatollah Khomeini and subscribe totally to his doctrine of making every Middle Eastern country an Islamic theocratic state. Our president rules this country firmly and will brook no opposition from these people. As long as he supports them, they leave us alone, for the time being—that is, as long as they are obsessed with terrorizing Israel. About the only support we can give here is to not let them get a foothold politically in our country. What more, I can't even begin to think. I know you must feel disappointed."

"No," Elie replied with disappointment in the voice, "the way you explain it shows that your approach is shrewd, and it at least prevents them from taking over a country whose government could be vulnerable to their terrorism. That is a big help even if it is not a contribution to our present mission. It is a great help to know that you and your president are sympathetic to our proposal."

They had arrived at the parking area just outside the Old City, so the conversation halted for the time being, but not before Elie got in a comment.

"Tariq, I understand what you have told me, but there is one thing you can do that will be of great help. But I had better wait till we get back to the house. I can't wait to see if this place has changed since my childhood. I can still smell the odors of the bazaars after all these years."

"Things haven't changed much. I don't need to tell you not to pay the first price they throw out at you. That's just the beginning of the game."

"I remember. That's part of the fun in these bazaars. Haggling is their way of life. In fact, I really think they are disappointed if you don't give them a hard time when you are buying something. It's part of their day's recreation."

"I think you're right, Elie. They do enjoy it, even the kids. It's fun watching them as they practice haggling with the old men."

"Tariq, look over here. That lady is selling saffron."

"Yes, it is widely used in cooking our rice."

"I know, but look at the price! I can't believe it is so cheap, only ten dollars for a kilo. That would sell for four or five hundred dollars back in the States. At that price, I'm going to get some for all my friends."

After wandering through the bazaar and visiting all the booths, Elie came across an old man selling gorgeous writing desks with inlaid mother-of-pearl set in precious light and dark wood. He could not resist haggling for two tables for his sisters. The old man smiled at Elie's shrewdness in beating him down on the price.

"You are good at this. Where did you learn to trade like you do?" the old man asked him.

"From practicing with my mother when I was young. And even when I got older, I still had to defend everything I did."

The man liked Elie's childlike love of fun and told him he would sell him the desks for even less than they had agreed upon. He also was surprised at Elie's fluency in Arabic.

"It was fun doing business with you, sir," Elie said as he began to walk away from the booth.

"Tariq, now that I have these two desks, how in heaven do I ship them home?"

"Don't you worry about that, Elie. I'll take care of that part for you. But you'll have to give me your sisters' names and addresses, so I'll know where to ship them."

"I'll write it out for you when we get back to the house. That is so kind of you. Can you find out the cost of the shipping so I can pay you before I leave?"

"We'll discuss that later."

Tariq arranged to have the carpenter prepare the desks for shipping and deliver them to his house by the next day; when the man read the card and realized whom he was dealing with, he was only too happy to agree. Elie and Tariq then drove back to the house to get ready for supper.

Rice flavored with lamb and a spicy blend of herbs cooked to perfection in grape leaves was the perfect end to a remarkable day. After supper, Tariq and his wife and son and two daughters retired with Elie to the deck outside the kitchen. The men had Arabic coffee, the women drank tea, and they all feasted on Turkish delights.

"Let us just enjoy this beautiful evening. It is too nice to be spoiled by politics," Tariq said, and all, especially the women, heartily agreed. The evening passed quickly, and so did the night's sleep.

Tariq and Elie rose early and discussed business before anyone else got up. By breakfast, they had finished their discussions. Tariq agreed to assist Elie in whatever way he could and gave Elie his private phone number. He could be of help with some of the more friendly Arab leaders. Elie could not have realistically expected more. He was wary enough of Middle Eastern politics to know that what Tariq was offering him was more than was expressed in words. He could now leave with a feeling of success in his first important political contact.

ELIE'S TRIP FROM DAMASCUS TO BEIRUT TOOK LONGER than he thought it would, as he had to drive through the mountains. It was not unpleasant, however. Lebanon is a beautiful country, so different from the desert lands he had just visited. Majestic trees lined the road through the mountains. The countryside was teeming with life, little children playing in the streets, donkey carts everywhere, with foreign cars, mostly Mercedes, zigzagging to avoid running down playing children or farmers delivering their goods on carts.

As Elie drove along the lonely roads, he was overcome with doubt, doubt about himself, his mission, his lack of professional training for this kind of delicate diplomacy. In the wake of these doubts he fell prey to a profound depression, which had a paralyzing effect on his enthusiasm to continue his mission. Should he turn back, bring the car back to his new friend, and fly home? It seemed mad to continue; the mission was certain to fail.

As these depressing thoughts flooded his consciousness, he

suddenly became aware of a presence near him and was shocked to see Joshua in the passenger's seat.

"Joshua, what are you doing here? How did you get here? How did you just appear? I thought you were in Washington."

Joshua laughed out loud at Elie's confusion and shock. It seemed Jesus enjoyed shocking people with his sudden appearances, like his appearance to the apostles on the night of the Resurrection, and his appearance to the two disciples walking on their way to Emmaus, and his appearance that night walking toward the apostles' boat on the Sea of Galilee.

"Elie, why do you doubt? You have been well prepared for this mission. Even though you may not be a professional diplomat, you have been prepared by my Father for a long time to perform this very difficult task. So do not give in to these doubts. They are the tricks of the devil. I am still in Washington. Why are you so surprised that I am here as well? Am I not everywhere? Can I not be here as well? I knew you were going through a dangerous crisis, Elie, so here I am to reassure you."

"I have been so blind. I should have known all along who you really are. My Lord, forgive me for my lack of faith. I am so grateful that you consider me to do an important work for you."

"Elie, I have always watched over you, even when you did not realize it. When you brought all those sandwiches and coffee to me when I was homeless in the streets with all the other homeless, I knew you had a deep faith with your kind heart. You touched all those people week after week as they looked forward to your coming to visit them. Now you need me in your loneliness, and I am here. But know now that even when you cannot see me, I am still near and know all that you are going through. So do not be afraid."

"I will always remember that, Joshua, and I am at peace."

"Elie, look ahead! Do you see that small group of men on the left side of the highway?"

"Yes."

"As you approach that spot in the road, turn off sharply into the field and then go back on the road again and move on as fast as you can."

As he approached the men, they looked like ordinary people, but Elie did as Joshua directed, pulling off the highway into the field, then turning back onto the highway again. As he passed the spot, Elie looked into the rearview mirror and saw the results of a huge explosion, with rock and dirt flying high into the air.

"Joshua, I am so glad you are with me! That could have been a disaster. Was that intended for me? Why? Who would have known about me, and what would I mean to them, anyway? And more frightening, who would have told them?"

"It was not any of your friends whom you visited. There are spies who monitor everything your friends do, and they are the ones responsible for what happened. But do not worry, as I am aware of everything, and I anticipate what they plan, so they cannot frustrate our plans. Elie, we are now approaching the city. On the first street corner, you will see a man standing there, watching this road. He is the contact who has been sent to meet you. They are not our kind of people, so be careful. And remember, you have two ears and two eyes and only one mouth. That is for a good reason. This is the time to watch and listen and say little. We need these people for the time being, so be gracious but wary, 'simple as a dove, but as sly as a fox.' Remember, I will be with you all along the way. So fear not."

"Sounds familiar, Joshua."

As they approached the intersection at the entrance to

Beirut, the man watched the car intently and then made a simple gesture of recognition. Elie pulled over to the side of the street. As he did, Joshua opened the door and got out so the stranger could take his seat. Then Joshua walked down the busy street and disappeared in the crowd.

"My name is Sayyed. I am an assistant to General Ahmed Chamoun, who sent me to escort you to his home."

"And I am Elie Zambaka. I have been sent by a man well known to General Chamoun. I look forward to meeting the general."

With Joshua gone, Elie's sense of security fled. Even though the stranger was supposedly a trusted ally, Elie could not be sure. Everything in this hateful part of the world was suspicion and had the smell of evil. There is no odor like the pungent stench of evil. Elie smelled it in Sayyed, and even though Joshua assured him he was his guide, as much as he trusted Joshua, he could not help but feel an almost paralyzing fear.

"I will take you to the general. You will be warmly welcomed by him and by our people, and I assure you, you need not fear anything."

The unctuous assurance made Elie even more suspicious. Why did Sayyed feel a need to assure him of his safety? He kept thinking of Joshua's reassurance. Now that he knew Joshua's real identity, he knew he had to trust him. This man might not be trustworthy, but Joshua must see beyond his potential for evil and know that for now he was just a harmless emissary. He felt he would see Joshua again. Did he not promise that he would be close by? Elie felt at peace. Down through back streets and dusty roads, passing dilapidated buildings, sad remains of not-so-recent conflicts, they drove.

"Turn left at the next corner and then sharply to the right and up the tree-lined road," Sayyed ordered.

Elie did as he was told.

The trees lining the road were majestic, like the Lombardy poplars of Italy, but these were more like tall, columnar cedars. This road was obviously a driveway, the approach to a villa, no doubt.

Elie's guess was right. At the end of the road, far up on the hill, was a sprawling villa, guarded by a veritable army of armed, uniformed guards. Elie dared not ask any questions. He just drank in everything with his eyes, missing nothing as they drove closer to the villa. He knew Joshua was close and that nothing would happen, but he was still frightened.

As they neared a security gate, two armed guards approached the car, and seeing Elie's escort, they asked him if everything was okay. When he assured them, they allowed the car to pass. Elie's heart was beating like a two-cylinder engine, ready to jump out of his chest.

At the front entrance to the mansion, more armed guards approached the car on both sides, double-checking the identity of the occupants, then opened the doors for them to get out. The two were welcomed and told to go inside. General Chamoun was expecting them.

Who was this General Chamoun? The only people with that name were friends, or at least collaborators, of Ariel Sharon when he was head of the armed forces. The one Elie knew had collaborated with Sharon in the massacre of the Palestinian women and children at the Shatila refugee camp. His heart froze. What was he getting into? Why had Ibrahim sent him to this godforsaken place all by himself? Why was he not accompanied by others more familiar with the people and their complex relationships? He felt so vulnerable and at everyone's mercy. Maybe this was the way Joshua wanted it to be. He thought so differently from everyone else. But then why wouldn't he, being who he was? His thoughts were not our thoughts, as far above us as the heavens. As much as Elie believed in Joshua, it still did not calm his panic. He was all alone in this dreadful region, where hatred and fear and greed poisoned the whole atmosphere. As he was ushered into the mansion, he could feel evil, and it almost smothered him. Beginning to hyperventilate, he felt as if he were going to faint and hoped it was not noticeable.

As they entered the large open entrance hall, a servant directed Elie into a library off to the left of the hall.

"If you would be so kind as to take a seat and make yourself at home, the general will be with you shortly," the servant instructed him, then withdrew and left Elie to his thoughts.

"Joshua, where are you when I need you?" Elie prayed in desperation. "I don't like it in this place. There is something diabolical about the whole atmosphere. I wish I could escape and run away. I'm afraid if I even do that, I'd be shot. Lord, help me. I am about to panic."

Of course, he did not expect an answer, though he was confident Joshua heard him. He could even sense him laughing quietly at Elie's discomfort, knowing that there was really nothing to fear, even though he was right about the evil surrounding the place. It was an evil that emanated from the general himself. Elie was right about his fear of even meeting him. But Joshua knew that at this particular time and under these circumstances, there was no cause for alarm.

When the general walked in, Elie stood up and the two men embraced in the ordinary Middle Eastern fashion. Elie felt he was embracing the devil, and his insides shivered.

"Mr. Zambaka, I had been expecting you. Your friends, and my friends, have communicated to me that you were on your way here, and I have been looking forward to meeting with you. Ibrahim has told me all about you. He holds you in great esteem, so I welcome you to my home as a friend of my dear friend."

"General, to meet you is, indeed, a most fascinating and intriguing experience."

"Fascinating and intriguing" were the only words Elie could think of at the moment to avoid telling a lie. His choices were not lost on the general; he immediately picked up his guest's uneasiness and attempted to put him in a more receptive frame of mind by explaining his difficult situation.

"It is not easy to live in this region. We Christians are surrounded by Muslims, and we have to be strong, personally and even militarily, so as not to be overwhelmed by circumstances that can so easily turn against us, as you probably know from your CNN news. You are Persian, are you not? Or Iranian, I should say—and a Christian as well, as Ibrahim informed me?"

"Yes, we left Iran for the United States many years ago, though we still have relatives and friends back here."

"You will be able to more easily understand our precarious position as leading Christians in such circumstances. Ibrahim explained a little of the mission he has committed to you. He must be very fond of you and respect you greatly to entrust you with such a delicate and, I must say, dangerous undertaking. Have you been doing this kind of diplomatic work for very long?"

Elie did not feel comfortable with the general. Everything he said made Elie feel more uncomfortable, as if his host were stripping him of whatever little confidence he had in himself and his ability to execute this mission successfully.

"No," Elie said in response to the general's question. "I know that Ibrahim is a wise and prudent man and felt that God could more easily use a person who did not have too much confidence in his personal abilities to do the job. He saw too many important people with big egos mess up some of his projects in the past and do things that were downright immoral or dishonest. He felt a simple person might be more open to God's guidance in a task that was so delicate, though I do not know why he asked me. Ibrahim said to me when I questioned him, 'Do not worry, Elie, God always chooses the weak ones of the world to accomplish his greatest works. So do not be afraid.' "

Elie knew that what he said was not very diplomatic, and the general's show of uneasiness made him realize that he wondered if Elie knew about his recent clandestine and not so honorable activities.

"I am sure Ibrahim made a good choice in sending you on this mission. Elie, can you tell me precisely what it is that you would like to accomplish while you are here?"

"I would be delighted, and then you will understand why Ibrahim felt it so important for me to meet with you and solicit your help. For decades now, overtures for peace have been made and discussed and feeble attempts made to move the efforts forward. However, no one really wanted to change the situation. The Israelis kept building new settlements on the West Bank, thus making a Palestinian state an impossibility. Muslim extremists were determined to drive the Israelis out of what they felt was their land. Their ancestors have lived there two thousand years.

"Back in Washington, a man came along and became friendly with Ibrahim and other important people of Arabic heritage, as well as Jewish people concerned about the crisis here, and this stranger, whose name is Joshua, convinced all of us that we could do something that could eventually bring about peace. After a number of meetings and discussions, as well as being detained by government agents, we all felt that we would make our own effort to influence important people here and see if we could not convince them that peace was in everyone's interest, especially their children's, if they had any real concern for their children. So here I am. And I am here to ask your help. I know you are a powerful Christian leader and many people look up to you, especially some powerful Israelis."

"What are you expecting of me, if I should be convinced that what you are undertaking is realistic?"

"I am not asking anything of you that would put you in any kind of compromising position. What I do need is an introduction to some of your close Israeli friends. Would you be willing to do that for me?"

"You must realize that I am an Arab, first of all. My Israeli friends are, as they realize, friends of convenience. When we can mutually help each other, we have an understanding that we will work together. But we are not allies. They are important to us in keeping the Syrians from interfering too much in our country, as they have in the past. But, yes, I think I could at least ask them if they would be willing to meet with you. That is the least I can do. Mr. Sharon and I have a good businesslike relationship, and I am sure I could convince him to lend his ear to what you have in mind. I am sure he also knows Ibrahim, and as his representative, you will be given a respectful hearing."

"Thank you, General. That is a big help, and that will bring me to the heart of the issue. Concerning your own country, is there anything here you might do that could be a help to our cause?"

"My dear Mr. Zambaka, that is an entirely different issue. Our country is very complicated. I am sure you are familiar with the political situation here. It is forty percent Catholic and sixty percent Muslim of various sects, and the situation is always fragile and tense. It is hard for any of us to make a move without being suspect. Since you just came from Damascus, I could introduce you to some of Mr. Hassan's people here. It is possible he may have contacted them already. I would be happy to arrange for you to meet them."

"That would be wonderful. If we could get a commitment from them to support us, others closer to the problem in Ramallah would be more open to listening to us. How about the Hezbollah leaders here?"

"Mr. Zambaka, I am beginning to understand why Ibrahim sent you on this mission. You are very thorough and don't even hesitate to ask for the impossible. You are now barging into territory where even angels dare not tread. What in God's name can the Hezbollah do to help you?"

"If I can convince them that peace is to their benefit, and that they can accomplish through peace what is ultimately impossible to attain through violence, they might be willing to put pressure on Yasser Arafat and the Palestinians to take the peace process seriously and negotiate in good faith with the Israelis."

"Arafat with Sharon?" General Chamoun said, surprised. "Impossible! Those two men hate each other with an undying bitterness, and they will never work together. Besides, Sharon is determined to continue building settlements on the West Bank to make sure the Palestinians cannot possibly put together a unified state. The West Bank is like a checkerboard."

"But it is still worth a try," Elie said with genuine humility in his voice.

"God must be with you, Mr. Zambaka. Only God can solve this problem. It is beyond any of us. But, yes, I can arrange for you to meet the Hezbollah leaders here. But we will have to wait until tomorrow morning to do that. Now let us get down to some serious business. As a Persian, you will no doubt feel at home with our food here. But what kind of wine do you like?"

"I am certain you are more a connoisseur of good wines than I. I know I will be pleased with whatever you serve."

"Well, this was a long session. I had not intended to go into business so abruptly, but I have to admit, you are a very engaging person, and you had me intrigued concerning your plans. Now that our business is over, we can enjoy the evening. Walk with me into my study, where you can meet some friends who just happen to be here for supper."

Although Elie knew none of the people in the room, as the evening wore on, he was stunned to see so many important, powerful people in one man's home, and just for dinner. As he became acquainted with each one over the course of the evening, he realized that many of these people were the very ones he was scheduled to meet. He then understood what Joshua meant when he'd said his next host was an important part of the plan. He was indeed.

"Well, Mr. Zambaka, are you pleased to meet our guests? You see I anticipated your request before you even explained to me the purpose of your visit. I took the liberty of inviting the very ones you wanted to meet to visit with us this evening. My respect and love for our mutual friend Ibrahim inspired me to do this for you. You probably do not know this, but Ibrahim and I are cousins. As children we played together, and although as adults our approach to important matters differs considerably, we still love each other dearly and never hesitate to help each other when we are needed. Now, dear friend, the rest is up to you."

"General, I am stunned. I am rarely lost for words, but tonight I am speechless. I cannot tell you the anxiety you spared me in trying to find these people. You surely are loyal to Ibrahim. I can't wait to tell him what you have done for us."

As the general left Elie and moved among his guests, Elie remembered Joshua's warning to look and listen and say little. But then how could he share his important mission with the very people he was supposed to meet? "Simple as a dove, sly as a fox," Joshua had said. How was he to interpret that for this evening? As he scanned the room, he noticed that the man standing a short distant away was a leader of the Hezbollah. The man talking with him was an assistant to Yasser Arafat. How had the general managed to get all these people to come to his house? Obviously, Middle Eastern politics was more complicated than Elie could have ever imagined.

He approached the two men and stood by quietly until they had finished talking.

"Good evening, gentlemen, I am Elie Zambaka. General Chamoun was kind enough to invite me to spend some time with him."

"It is a pleasure meeting you. This is Abdullah Pahkouri, and I am Mohammed Kyubi. We have been friends for many years. Welcome to our country. Your name, is it not Iraqi, or is it Persian?"

"Our family were businessmen in Persia, Iran. We left Iran when I was a child, but I still have fond memories of long ago. Lebanon is a beautiful country. Its people have always been progressive, far ahead of most other countries in the area. I notice there are still traces of Lebanon's former grandeur. Hopefully everything will one day be restored to what it was before all the problems."

"You remember what it was like?"

"I returned here often as I grew up, mostly on business. I always enjoyed my visits."

"We were told you have come here on a most important mission. Would you like to share it with us?" asked Mr. Kyubi.

"I would be happy to, but I would like to talk to each of you personally. There are many questions I have, and not being very knowledgeable in so many things, I need the advice of many of you. I think this could best be done in quiet, one-on-one talks. I really would like to respect each one's privacy, which would be difficult if we talk openly right now."

"That makes good sense, Mr. Zambaka. I am sure most of us will be quite willing to be of assistance," said Mr. Pahkouri.

As Elie walked through the group, he was surprised when he learned the identity of each person and the organizations to which each belonged. He began to feel guilty for having judged General Chamoun so harshly but still wondered why he felt he was in the presence of evil when he approached the villa.

Supper turned out to be just a gathering of friends having a meal together. Conversation was light. Any business had already been discussed during the extended cocktail hour. Elie enjoyed himself and even began to have a cordial feeling toward his host. He certainly did not seem like an evil man, but then Joshua had warned him to be very careful. If these people were evil, they were most polished in their cordiality and certainly gracious toward one another and to their guests. A good number of them were professionals, doctors, lawyers, engineers, and computer scientists. If they were evil, they were smooth and had transformed evil into a highly technological operation.

Elie realized he was letting down his guard and knew that if he did not stick to Joshua's advice, he could fall into traps that his overly gracious host might be setting for him. When the evening ended, he felt a deep sense of relief.

"Well, Mr. Zambaka, did you enjoy your evening?" the general asked him when all the guests had left.

"General Chamoun, I have never met a more gracious host. You are a man of rare class and good taste. I know you went through much trouble to bring all these people here, and I cannot tell you how grateful I am. You made my work very easy. I had been so worried about wandering around Lebanon looking for these people, and here you have them assembled all in one room."

"Now you can get a good night's sleep and not have to worry about tomorrow. Our priest will be coming here for liturgy at midmorning. If you would like to visit our little chapel, you are welcome. It is dedicated to Theotokos, the Mother of God. This is a title we have been celebrating in our country since the fourth century. After liturgy we will have a breakfast in honor of Jesus' mother."

"Thank you, General, I would love to attend liturgy with your family."

"You have had a long day, so sleep well, and don't worry about coming down early. The early morning commotion in the house will wake you early enough."

THE GENERAL WAS RIGHT. THE CHANGE OF GUARDS IN-
volved noisy cars coming and going at an early hour. It
was impossible to sleep in. Besides, Elie was impatient to see
what the day would bring. He was looking forward to liturgy,
as the Eastern rites called their Mass. He had attended the ancient rites long ago, but for a child the ceremonies were too
long. Now he was curious and looking forward to taking part
as an adult.

After showering and shaving, he found his way to the private chapel and was impressed with its beauty. It was a tiny architectural gem. For a man supposedly as evil as he assumed the
general to be, this was a remarkable testimony to a faith of some
sort, maybe a faith too well hidden and kept separate from his
life. There are many people like that. Religion is merely a compartment of life and in no way influences how they treat people. So they justify all their injustices and cruelty and destroying

of others' lives and reputation as just the way the world works. If you want to survive, you destroy others before they destroy you. Then they practice their worship of God as if it is merely another compartment of their life. Maybe that is the way the general is, Elie thought as he knelt on the prie-dieu to pray. He noticed two ladies with black veils over their heads, praying the rosary. An old man sat in a chair just looking up at the tabernacle, his lips moving as if conversing rather than praying, almost as if he were arguing or pleading with God rather than praying. Elie learned later that it was the general's father, himself once a powerful man, now feeble and crippled with arthritis.

The chapel was different from most American churches. A panel separating the altar from the main body of the chapel was beautifully decorated with icons of ancient fathers of the church: St. Ignatius of Antioch, St. John Chrysostom, St. Athanasius, the prophet Elias, and, in a prominent place, Theotokos, the image of Mary, Mother of God. As Elie prayed, his gaze focused on Mary, and in a moment he was overcome with a profound sense of a presence sitting in the chair next to him. Looking over, he saw no one, but he heard a gentle voice speaking to him: "Elie, my son, your mission is a difficult one, but do not be afraid, as my son has told you. I have come to comfort you. I know your mother has left you very much alone, and you miss her still. Would you like to be with her, Elie? She knows I am speaking to you, and she would feel much more at peace if you were with her. Would you like that?"

Elie was overwhelmed and thought he was going crazy, yet he was not in any turmoil. In fact, the words made him feel at peace. It was true that he missed his mother terribly since she died a number of years ago, but to leave this world and go there was a frightening thought. Life had been very painful and too complicated for this gentle soul. If this was Jesus' mother, and she was offering him a chance to go to heaven, how much more certainty would he want that he would go there?

"Mother Mary, I don't know whether this is all real or just my mind playing tricks on me, but if this is possible, I would not mind being with God and seeing my mother again. I miss her so much, and not a day passes that I don't shed tears over her absence."

"Continue with your mission, my son, and go on without fear. No one can really do you harm. All must be accomplished. I am so glad my son has chosen you to be his partner in this difficult work, but as you know, his planning is flawless. So trust him. Also, know that your mother is smiling on you."

Just then the chapel bell rang. The presence left just as simply as it had come, and Elie became aware that the chapel had filled with people while he was absorbed in his experience. Was it real? Had he fallen asleep and dreamed what seemed to him so real, or had it really happened? Whatever it was, it left him with a profound sense of peace, and any fear and doubt he had about his mission left him.

Last to enter the chapel was the general, his wife, and his children, with guards following them. The family walked up the short aisle and sat in the front, in seats reserved for them. The guards remained at the back of the chapel and stationed themselves at the entrance and at the back corners of the chapel, ready for any unforeseen incident.

The priest conducted all the ceremonies in Aramaic, the language Jesus spoke. Elie was overcome with emotion during this exotic liturgy. Although the service was long, it was in its own way simple and deeply moving, especially the ancient music and the sermon about Jesus' mother, which touched Elie as the priest described the event that took place so many centuries before, when the assembled bishops decided once and for all that Mary could indeed be called the Mother of God, since the person she gave birth to was a divine person. And he then went on to describe the wild jubilation of the populace as they paraded through the streets of the city, singing with joy. The priest also explained how Mary became *our* Mother as well, when we were baptized and became brothers and sisters of Jesus. For the first time, Elie felt a special closeness to Mary that brought him comfort in the fear and loneliness he was feeling on this strange mission.

The breakfast after the liturgy was a festive occasion and would have rivaled a Christmas celebration in Western countries. But after breakfast Elie was in a hurry to contact all the people the general had so graciously assembled for him the previous evening. Before leaving, he spent a few minutes with the general, expressing his deep gratitude for all that he had done for him in such a short time. The general promised to contact others among his Israeli friends and ask that they accept Elie with open minds.

After leaving the villa, Elie went first to see a man who had impressed him greatly at dinner. Eliah Mahmoud was in appearance a stately gentleman with gracious manners, an engineer by profession and one of the most powerful leaders of the Hezbollah. Elie had previously thought the Hezbollah to be nothing but a ragtag gang of murderers. Maybe they were, but this man certainly did not seem like a murderer. Elie wondered why a man of such learning and refinement would be involved in an organization notorious for its hate-filled murders of innocent people, among them little children.

Elie was surprised to find that his contact lived in a fashionable neighborhood and not some rat-infested hovel with a nest of other terrorists. When Elie arrived he was warmly welcomed and not treated with suspicion or a wary silence, as he expected.

"Mr. Zambaka, thank you for coming. I was expecting you. From our conversation last evening, I thought you might be interested in visiting with some of my colleagues, so I took the liberty of inviting them to spend some time with us after we have had a little private time for ourselves. Come right in, Mr. Zambaka, and don't feel like a stranger in my home."

Elie could not believe the treatment, after all the newspaper and TV accounts of kidnapped Americans held hostage and treated so cruelly. That was one of the things that he feared most, being taken hostage, held in isolation, and tortured on a daily basis. He was now beginning to realize the power and influence Ibrahim had in this place of contradictions.

"Would you like tea or Arabic coffee, Mr. Zambaka?"

"I think the coffee might be better, thank you."

"Fatima," the host called out to his wife, "would you please bring us some coffee and cakes?"

"I like your home, Mr. Mahmoud. It has been put together in good taste."

"Thank you. You were probably expecting that I live with some of those rough, unkempt characters you see on your American TV."

"As a matter of fact, I was," Elie replied with an embarrassed grin. "I was pleasantly surprised to meet such a refined and highly educated gentleman. I am sure you are the one who drew the plans for this beautiful home."

"Yes, it was my wife's dream to have a home like this, and I tried to plan everything the way she would like it. I admit I also like the way it is laid out. It is very practical and welcoming at the same time. Now, I know you have not come to talk about my house. I am sure you are reluctant to ask personal questions, so I will anticipate you by explaining my life and my philosophy, so you will understand what you can and cannot expect from me, and from my friends also, I may add.

"I was not born a terrorist, nor do I consider myself one. I live in a land that has been ours for over two thousand years. We Arabs are also the children of Abraham, and as Abraham's children, we also claim this land as our birthright. We do not deny the right of Israelis to live in the land of Palestine with us, but they have always considered Arabs as the bastard children of Abraham. We, of course, believe we are Abraham's true children, just as they are, and that we have our rights as his children just as they do. There are some radicals who would like to drive all the Israelis into the sea. I do not share that idea. They have suffered much, and there is plenty of room for us all to live in peace together.

"However, there are some radical Israelis, too, who would drive all Arabs out of the land, and they have in fact pretty much done that, as I will show you tomorrow when I take you to visit the refugee camps. The Israelis now have seventy-eight percent of the land, and our fifty percent has now been reduced to twenty-two percent, and even that twenty-two percent is cut up with tens of thousands of Israeli settlers living throughout our territory. Little by little, we will have nothing left. So the question is, what do we do? Sit by idly while the Israeli government builds more settlements and effectively drives us all out into refugee camps along the borders of Syria and Jordan and Lebanon? Our people are desperate. The neighboring countries don't want us. They are too poor to support us. Nor do we want to be in other countries. We want our own property back, property that has been in our family's possession for over two thousand years.

"People ask, 'Why do you kill innocent people?' And I ask,

'Who is innocent?' Are they innocent people who come in and take our land and live in settlements where our families had lived for almost two thousand years, and where they had their homes and olive groves, our heritage from our ancient ancestors? Just because they are not in military uniform does not mean they are not collaborators in the raping of our homeland. Are they not just as guilty as the soldiers who destroy our homes and drive us into refugee camps? Half of my family was killed by Menachem Begin's terrorist gang many years ago to make room for Israeli settlers. So you see, Mr. Zambaka, this is not a simple problem. It is quite complicated."

Elie was taken aback by the passion that exploded from a man of such refinement. He had seemed so calm on the surface, but that calm hid the volcano that raged not too far beneath the surface. Elie was frightened at the violence of his emotion.

"Mr. Mahmoud, you have revealed a whole new world to me. My heart hurts to hear of all the tragedy you and your family and others have suffered through the past half century. I appreciate your sharing with me your experiences."

"Now, Mr. Zambaka, what was it that brought you across the world to talk with me and my colleagues?"

"As you know and can easily tell from my name, I am an Arab, or at least a Persian. I have come—or, more precisely, I have been asked by Ibrahim Abboud and our group to come—on this trip alone not to ask for anything, but to share concerns about our people. There are many Arabs in America who feel so helpless as they see young Arab children killing themselves each day in an attempt to kill Israelis and wonder how fathers and mothers can allow such terrible things, especially when it is only the children and never adults who destroy themselves. They wonder what kind of men can talk little children into blowing themselves up when the men do not have the courage to do such a horrendous thing. Some of our more religious Muslim people cannot understand it because suicide is forbidden in the Koran.

"It is not that they do not sympathize with the goals of intifada, but they wonder whether all this waste of the best of our youths will accomplish what the sheiks and imams want to accomplish. And does it not destroy the best and most noble of our children, thus depriving our future nation of the benefit of our most dedicated young people?

"We watch the news about our families here and wonder if it will ever end. All these years of fighting and nothing has been accomplished but the slow destruction of all our resources. The Israelis have unlimited resources to completely destroy all our people, and though they may not do it openly, they can accomplish over a period of time what would be judged by the world as genocide if done too quickly. We know that were it not for the United Nations and other relief organizations our people would starve to death and die of exposure. And those of us who are educated are familiar with the experience of the Indian people who fought the British for decades and accomplished nothing. What wars and assassinations over many years could not accomplish, one lone voice of a simple old man accomplished by his strategy of reason and nonviolent resistance, and in the process he gained the admiration and support of the whole world. Perhaps Mr. Gandhi's strategy would be of benefit in this situation.

"I have come to ask if this is not an approach that could be more effective than having the best of our young people killing themselves—often to destroy the lives of decent and innocent Israelis, many of whom had at one time been your supporters against hateful radical groups in their own communities?"

The response was silence, a silence that Elie could not interpret. Mr. Mahmoud said nothing, not one word. Then, after what seemed an eternity, he spoke. "Mr. Zambaka, I think it is about time for my colleagues to come and hear what you have to say." Not another word was said between the two men, nor could Elie ascertain what was going through the man's complex mind. His wife had brought in the coffee and cakes, and sensing the silence, she put the tray on the coffee table and discreetly withdrew. The two men sat and nibbled on the cakes. The only sound was the sipping of the hot coffee. Elie was too uneasy to say anything, even to ask a question. Obviously his host was a deeper thinker than Elie had surmised. He could tell the man was pondering deeply what he had just expressed. He seemed impressed with the innocent simplicity of Elie's pained compassion for the sad plight of their people and his condemnation of the callous, cowardly cynicism of such sick men who would send children to their deaths while they watched with glee the destruction that followed. Elie was beginning to feel more positive about Mr. Mahmoud's silence. He could tell he was in deep thought, and perhaps feelings of personal shame, but he did not seem to be offended by what Elie had said.

In a short time, the other men began to appear at the house. Mrs. Mahmoud directed them to the parlor.

"Oh, you are here already! That did not take long," Mr. Mahmoud exclaimed. Elie stood as the men entered and introduced themselves, then took seats while waiting for the others to arrive. Within a few minutes, all those invited were present.

"Well, gentlemen, I appreciate your coming on such short notice. I think you will enjoy meeting our most unusual guest. I have already had my introduction to him and his purpose in coming here, but I will let him speak for himself.

"Mr. Zambaka, it is all yours now."

"I am grateful to all of you for coming this morning. As you can tell by my name, I am one of you, although I am Christian. I understand and feel your pain and frustration, and also your disillusionment with the world's politicians, who for the most part make no attempt to understand the desperate plight of our people here.

"Mr. Mahmoud and I have had a wonderful exchange of ideas and experiences; I hope we can have the same. I come here, as you may have already heard, not of my own initiative, but as one sent by a dear friend of all of you, Ibrahim Abboud. A short while ago, a group of us were assembled at the behest of a man who gathered Ibrahim and over seventy-five others to discuss the desperation of people in this area. This man made a profound impression on all of us, and we met on a number of occasions to discuss what we could do to influence in some small way a change for the better in the lives of our families and relatives here. This man will be visiting you soon, I am sure. I am just his forerunner, sent by Mr. Abboud to prepare for his coming.

"Permit me to share with you some thoughts as seeds for discussion. As you know, there are many of your friends and relatives back in the United States who are deeply concerned about the welfare of all of you. For years we have felt helpless to do anything to ease the pain of our people's desperate situation. It breaks our hearts seeing children being sent out to blow themselves up as a way of defending your people and your homeland. We have been meeting and discussing what we could do to help. As the intifada seems to be unproductive and merely wastes our young children's lives, and the Israeli response brings on even more destruction, we would like to offer our help and whatever influence our people have to work for a solution to this tragic situation."

At that point, one of the group interrupted Elie.

"What is your name, sir?"

"My name is Ahmed, Ahmed Habbani. I am in charge of the Hezbollah in southern Lebanon. What makes you think that you and your friends in America are wiser than those of us who have been living in the midst of this destruction of our country and our people?"

"Mr. Habbani, I am sure we are not wiser. We certainly do not have the depth of knowledge you have been experiencing here on a daily basis. What Mr. Abboud and his friends would like to offer is the personal influence they have because of their network of business connections throughout this whole region. Those of you who know these men know how shrewd they are not only in business, but also in hammering out workable arrangements in difficult financial situations. Politics is no different. There are also important Jewish people in our group of friends who are willing to use their influence with various important Israelis. Together we may be able to help bring about a solution. We would at least like to try."

"I'm not very impressed. In fact, I think you are meddling in something of which you are all ignorant."

"We may be ignorant of many things that happen here, but our friends' contacts here, I assure you, are most valuable and are in a more accommodating position than soldiers in the field, or street fighters, with whom an enemy is loath to deal. Businessmen have their own language and their own values and their own approach to solving seemingly insoluble problems."

As Elie continued to persuade the men to accept the proposal, he could see their resistance. Even though their guerrilla tactics had been ineffective, they were still unwilling even to think of an alternative. He could also see that a couple of the men were downright hostile toward everything he said and would in the end oppose any attempt to interfere in what they felt was their war; they would fight their war in whatever way they chose.

As the discussion was becoming heated, and some hotheads even threatened violence to prevent any interference, Mr. Mahmoud, who was the most important and most powerful of all the leaders present, spoke out in Elie's defense.

"Gentlemen, I expected to hear differences of opinion to Mr. Zambaka's proposals, but I am surprised at the expressions of hostility toward a guest in my home and a person sent by someone for whom we all have the greatest respect. My feeling is, and I expect you to consider it wisely, that Mr. Zambaka should bring back to Mr. Abboud a positive response and let their people use whatever influence they may have to meet and discuss with important individuals on both sides and see if they can do any good. If they can, all well and good. If they fail, well, nothing has been lost."

By the end of the meeting, not everyone was pleased, but they agreed to discuss with their own people the proposals that were offered. Mr. Mahmoud invited them all to stay for lunch, which had a much more cordial atmosphere than the meeting, though some men were still opposed to any interference in their long, painful struggle by people who did nothing more than sit in front of their televisions and concoct armchair solutions to something of which they were totally ignorant. Even Elie could see their point of view. His trump card was that these armchair meddlers still had entrée to the most important people on both sides and were in a much better position to hammer out a solid business deal. After all, were not most political issues ultimately resolved by good business deals?

This was not the last of Elie's meetings with these people. He knew the hardliners were on the spot in front of others, afraid to show any willingness to compromise. He would see them again, alone. He felt his host was a reasonable man. He had four children of his own, three of them boys, all of whom he loved dearly and would not sacrifice no matter what the cause. Elie knew he could count on him, and he was the important one.

Elie left Mr. Mahmoud's house shortly after lunch and visited two of those who had been present and who he sensed needed more discussion. It took him almost an hour to find where they lived, so well hidden were their homes. It took the best part of the afternoon to make them at least understand the reasonableness of his position, though when he left he knew he had not succeeded in persuading either of them to accept his position. In the end, he left them both with what he felt was an appreciation of his sincere concern for their interests. But fanatics trust least of all those whose hearts are true, since such people can always be counted on to do the right thing. And to fanatics, people who need to do the right thing will always be undependable and a potential threat to their nefarious schemes.

He moved on to Beiteddine, some thirty miles southeast of Beirut. It is an old village, with a magnificent palace reflecting late Lebanese architecture perched on top of a hill over 2,500 feet above the village. Much of the palace and its precious contents had been destroyed by the Israelis during the recent war.

Having arrived there, Elie spent some time trying to find his contacts. He finally tracked them down and met with each of them separately. They were most difficult individuals, hard men whose souls were seared by personal tragedy. Not only had their families lost their homes and all their possessions when original Zionist armies killed their parents and grandparents, they had also seen two of their children killed by careless Israeli gunfire as they played in the streets. Their hatred of Israelis was implacable. They were part of the group that vowed never to rest until they had driven out every last Israeli from their homeland and won back the land the Israelis had stolen from them. Elie listened patiently. It was neither his place nor his purpose to accept or deny their accounts of historical events, whether he agreed or disagreed with what they had to say. It was his place only to listen. And for Elie, that was difficult. Perhaps Mr. Mahmoud could have some influence over them at a later time.

When he left them he had a sick feeling in the pit of his stomach. That night, he slept in a cheap hotel and rested little, as he feared anything could happen. He was beginning to fear assassination and was finding it difficult to trust anyone, especially in this area where there was so much hatred. The next day he woke up early, at sunrise, and had a breakfast of cheese, eggs, leeks, pita bread, and black coffee.

Knowing it would be difficult to cross from Lebanon into Israel, Elie phoned ahead and spoke to an official at the Israeli Department of State, a woman whom Ibrahim knew and had already contacted. When Elie called she had been expecting him, and after giving him directions as to which checkpoint to approach, she contacted the officer in charge of the checkpoint and directed him to guarantee Elie safe passage and an escort to Haifa.

When Elie arrived at the checkpoint, he was delighted with the courtesy shown him by the officer in charge, who immediately arranged an escort to Haifa, where Elie was to spend the day at the Carmelite monastery on Mount Carmel, the site of the prophet Elias's haunt while he was on bad terms with King Ahab and half the distrusting population, which at the time had converted to pagan gods.

Elie felt like an important diplomat as the escort with sirens blowing and lights flashing sped along the highways and through crowded streets.

The officers dropped him off at the monastery, then walked across the street to the former monastic building now used as a radar site, to explain their presence in the area and report back to the woman official at the State Department who had originally given them their instructions.

Elie was received warmly at the monastery, as he had visited there before and made friends with the monks. He asked if he might see his friend and namesake, Father Elias Friedman, a Jewish war hero who fought in the Jewish uprising in Warsaw. Elie had once supported his application for Israeli citizenship, which was denied by the Israeli Supreme Court because he had converted to Catholicism.

Elie had been hoping to see Father Elias and talk over many things that had transpired through their years of separation. However, he was shocked to find out that he had recently died. The brother who met him escorted him to his room and, after dropping off what little luggage he had, brought him down to the refectory, as they called the dining room, and served him a light afternoon snack, then went to inform the prior, the monk in charge, of Elie's arrival.

"Elie," the prior said on entering the refectory, "it has been quite a while since your last visit. Brother Anselm probably told you of Elias's death. It was a profound loss to all of us. He was a saintly man who inspired our whole community, even the Arabs among us. He had spoken much about all you had done for him in the past. For that you will always be a most welcome guest in our monastery. And if you ever get the urge to take Elias's place and join our community, we would all welcome you with open arms."

"Thank you, Father, I feel honored, even though I feel so bad about Father Elias's death. He *was* a good priest, and I am sure he's in heaven. It is too bad he was never allowed to become an Israeli citizen. It meant so much to him, especially since he was a war hero."

"While you are here, Elie, is there anything we can do for you?"

"Yes, I would love to visit the shrine of my patron saint, the prophet Elias. Father Elias took me to the shrine once before, but I have forgotten the pathway to it and to the caves where Elias sheltered while hiding from the king."

"I will take you myself. It's not far, just down the path behind the monastery. We can go either after supper or tomorrow morning."

"I think I'd prefer to go after supper. I may have to leave tomorrow. I'm really here in the country on an important mission, which I would like to talk to you about after dinner."

"Good, we can talk on our way to the shrine. Why don't you rest up now and make yourself at home. I'll see you at supper."

The guest room was the same as the monks' rooms. Elie felt very much at home, but the memory of his last visit with Father Elias haunted him. He was so much alive then and had so many things he wanted to accomplish. How could he be dead? And he never obtained his lifelong dream, to become an Israeli citizen. Elie fell on his bed and wept.

ELIE AND THE PRIOR WALKED ALONG THE PATH TO THE shrine of the prophet Elias. It had been a long time since he had visited this place sacred to his namesake.

"Do you know the story of our founder, Elie?" the monk asked him.

"Father Elias told me the story a long time ago, but I have forgotten most of the details. The part I do remember is the time he spent in the cave overlooking the sea, as he waited for Yahweh to give him a sign. He experienced all kinds of violent things in nature and did not find God, but then a gentle breeze passed the entrance to the cave, and Elias recognized the presence of Yahweh in the gentle breeze. Then he saw an immaculate white cloud in the shape of a foot rise out of the sea, and that immaculate white cloud was the harbinger of the life-giving rains that finally came after six long years of drought and famine."

"You have a good memory, my friend. It was at that time that Elias had gathered holy men around him who continued to live in those caves that dot the mountainside. That was the beginning of our community. Many years later, Jesus and his mother visited here, and our ancestors have been dedicated to the Messiah and his mother ever since."

"That is why I feel so close to your order," Elie interjected, "because it goes back to our ancient roots and was dedicated to the Messiah and his mother right from the start."

"Elie, times are very difficult here lately. Are you sure you want to wander around in places where there is so much danger?"

"This time I have come for a reason. I have been sent on a mission. I hope you and the monks will pray for its success. I have been sent by some very influential people back home to meet and talk to Arab and Israeli leaders in the hope of fostering peace. Would you have any suggestions as to whom I should visit?"

"Let me think. . . . Yes, I have a very good person who could be of great help. His name is the same as yours. He is the founder of the first peace movement here and has Jews and Arabs working together to promote peace. He is a powerful force for peace in the country. His name is Elias Chacour. He is a priest in the Melkite rite. He lives in a small town in Galilee. I will look up the exact address for you before you leave."

"Perfect. That will be a big help."

Arriving at the shrine of the prophet Elias, the two men paused for a moment in deep thought as they meditated on the troubled times the prophet faced, times not much different then from now. Elie's prayer was for guidance and strength, as the prophet had prayed for so long ago.

"May the holy prophet guide you, Elie, on your difficult mission, and ask the Lord to touch those with hard hearts and hardened spirits."

"Amen to that, Father. Tomorrow morning I leave. I know I can count on the monks' prayers for God to touch people's hearts."

"You will be in our prayers every day. This place of prayer is unusual. Arabs and Jews come here to visit the shrine of the prophet Elias. Sometimes we even see some of them praying together. We see that God does touch people's hearts, and in ways that touch our hearts."

The men walked back to the monastery. The monks' prayers that evening were fervent pleas for Elie's safety and for peace in their troubled country.

After liturgy and breakfast, Elie was anxious to continue his journey. He followed the prior's directions to Elias Chacour's residence in Galilee, hardly an hour's ride from Mount Carmel. The scenery was beautiful along the way, though the roads were busy with early morning rush-hour traffic.

Trying to find Elias Chacour's residence turned out not to be as easy as Elie had thought it would be. Ibillin, the village where he lived and worked, was not even on the map. Many people in the area did not even know where it was. Finally, a gas station attendant who lived in the village laughed at Elie's confusion.

"Don't get discouraged. It's a real place. I live there," he told him. "The Israelis do not put it on their maps because the politicians are not happy with us. You will see that Ibillin is quite advanced. It has a school with four thousand students, Jews, Arabs, and Christians. We are now getting ready to build a university for the students. This makes the politicians furious because we all live in harmony and peace, which shows it can be done and proves they really don't want peace."

Ibillin was not much farther. As Elie entered the village, it was like going into another country. The people were warm and friendly. He immediately asked a pedestrian where he could find Abuna Chacour, *abuna* being the Arab equivalent of the Jewish *abba,* "father," which is what the Arabs called their priest. Father Chacour was at the school up on the hillside at the time, so Elie took the liberty of visiting the sprawling complex, a phenomenon hard to imagine in a Palestinian area.

Elie was surprised to see a gentle, cordial man. He had expected a high-energy person, businesslike, someone with no time to waste.

"You must be Elie Zambaka. I was told that you might be coming to visit our little village. You are most welcome," the priest said as he gave him a warm Arab hug.

"Father Chacour, you caught me off guard. You are so friendly and down-to-earth. I expected a high-pressure businessman."

"No, I am just a simple priest trying to make our little village a happy place in which to live and grow in peace. It is a busy place, especially with our flourishing school. Would you like me to give you a little tour?"

"I would love that."

As they walked through the vast complex, Elie was impressed not only with the size of the operation and the number of students now attending the college, but at how well the Arab and Jewish students socialized, even walking together in small groups as friends.

"You see, it can be done," the priest said with pride, "and as Christians following Jesus' Sermon on the Mount, and his teaching of forgiveness, we can show the way by our example. Yes, it does work."

After the tour, they ended in the rectory.

"Father, I read your book, *Blood Brothers*. Is this the same rectory where you were first assigned?"

"Yes, and I have been here ever since, almost forty years. A lot has happened in those forty years, a lot of tragedy and a lot more of hope. My coming here was a shock. My parishioners had a bad experience with the former pastor, so I wasn't accepted at first. I'll never forget the first Easter ceremony. I was determined to get my people to realize that they were not Christians in the way they treated one another, so after the Easter mass, I went down to the back of the church and locked the door so no one could get out. Then I told them that we were going to stay there until they all made peace with one another. The first one to respond was the chief of police, who had not talked to his brother in years and did not even tell him when their mother had died. He was the first one to walk across the aisle and hug his brother and ask for forgiveness. When the others saw that, they all broke down and made peace with family and neighbors whom they had not talked to for many years. It was a beautiful thing to witness. Since then, peace and reconciliation has been the theme of my whole ministry as a priest."

"I have to admit, I am deeply impressed with all you have accomplished."

"It is not I who have accomplished this dream. We have all worked together, and people of other countries have been most generous. They see the good that has been done, and they understand the obstacles that have been put in our way by the government, so they are more determined than ever to see that we succeed, as they realized it benefits everyone, Jews and Arabs alike.

"It was difficult in the beginning. People in the area were

demoralized and angry. Ibillin is an Arab village, half Muslim, half Christian. The villagers are an agglomeration of what remained from four different villages that were destroyed and the population deported. Those who fled the deportation and hid later agglomerated themselves here and became a large village of eighty-five hundred inhabitants. These are among the four hundred and sixty towns and villages that were completely destroyed or deleted or emptied for the arrival of the émigrés."

As Elie and the priest entered the kitchen, the cook greeted them and began setting out a tray of cheese and pita bread and olives and a bottle of wine made by one of the neighbors. As both were busy to get on with their work, they wasted no time in getting to the point of Elie's visit.

"My friend, you came for a purpose. I know you need to meet some important people. I have an appointment in ten minutes, so I'll be brief. I have some very influential Israeli friends who have been quietly working with me for years. They are quite wealthy and have dedicated their lives to bringing peace to this troubled land. They are a credit to their people. As I knew you were coming, I put their names and addresses and phone numbers on a sheet of paper with directions to their homes or places of business. You should have no trouble finding them. I will contact them in the meantime and make them aware of your coming. I am sure they will welcome you. May the good Lord bless you and protect you on your way. You will be in my prayers. And may God grant success to your mission."

He took the sheet of paper out of the pocket of his cassock and gave it to Elie.

There was little Elie could say other than a simple "Thank you so much for being so gracious to me, even though I barged in on your very busy schedule. I am most grateful for your help. These contacts are probably the most important of all I will have to meet."

With that the two men parted. Elie turned and kissed the cook on both cheeks, thanking her for her hospitality. She blushed.

As Elie entered his car, he scanned the list the priest had given him. One man lived in Haifa, so that would be his first stop. It was not far from Mount Carmel, which he had just left. But as the address was southeast of the city, it would not be a long drive. The man's name was Sharon. Elie wondered if he was a relative of the prime minister. This would be very interesting. Mrs. Sharon's name was also on the list. The two must work together in the peace movement.

The trip did not take long. Elie called from the satellite phone his benefactor had left in the car for his use. Mrs. Sharon was at home and had already been apprised of his coming. Her husband would be back in about an hour, as he had business to attend to. She assured Elie his visit would be most welcome.

The Sharons' residence was a modest home in a nice upscale development. One could tell they were not pretentious people, even though Elie could sense they were people of means and influence.

As he parked his car and exited, he was met at the front door by an attractive woman seemingly in her early forties. She welcomed Elie most cordially and escorted him into the living room.

"My husband just called. He is on his way home and should be here in a few minutes," she informed Elie. "As Abuna Chacour probably told you, my husband and I both work together in the peace movement. Our part, though, is done quietly, as a relative is high up in the government."

Elie smiled, realizing his hunch was correct: The couple *was* related to the prime minister.

"You have been on quite a journey, I was told. It must have been a most exciting adventure. I hope you did not run into any mishaps along the way. This kind of peace work is dangerous. There are so many who want peace efforts to fail. Radicals on both sides won't rest until the others are driven out of the country. You are fortunate, Mr. Zambaka, to have arrived here in one piece."

"It has been quite pleasant for the most part. Only one close call. That was on the way to Damascus. Some group must have been informed of my whereabouts, and they detonated a bomb as I approached their position. Fortunately, I was able to avoid the explosion. But it was a good wake-up call. I finally realized this was not a game. These people mean business. Since then I have been much more wary of what might happen."

"Oh, here comes Moshe, I hear his car in the driveway."

Moshe Sharon was a big man, much like his relative, effusive, ebullient, and direct, saying what was on his mind. As he entered, his voice boomed through the house: "Iris, I see that radical peacemonger arrived already."

"We're in the living room, dear."

When he entered, Elie stood up to greet him. Moshe's hug almost broke him in half. He had the strength of a bull.

"Welcome to our home, friend. I hope your trip here was pleasant. I already have reports of your journey. We have a very good intelligence network."

"Yes, the trip was uneventful for the most part. I did meet some interesting people along the way. They have all been very helpful. As you can see, my own intelligence led me right to your doorstep. You have quite a reputation. I must say, you look very much like a gentleman I would see frequently on TV back in the United States."

"You have a good sense of humor, young man. Yes, we are cousins. We used to play together when we were kids, but now we play a rough game of chess together. We are both dedicated to our different causes, and we both respect each other, knowing where we both came from, but, well, we will discuss those matters more at length later on."

The Sharons and Elie became fast friends. They immediately understood each other and could in turn be serious and humorous and enjoy each other's repartee. Elie was there longer than he intended, primarily because they were having such a good time together. As the afternoon wore on, Moshe told Elie he might as well stay for supper and spend the evening, as there wasn't much he could do once it grew dark. Elie did not need much encouragement and gladly agreed to spend the night.

The time after supper was the most fruitful. Moshe and Iris informed Elie of all the work they had been doing and what they had been able to accomplish so far in pushing for moderation and reason in resolving the turmoil in the country. Moshe phoned a few of his collaborators who lived nearby and invited them over to meet Elie. They were all interested in Elie's mission and curious as to what he hoped to accomplish. Elie explained in detail how their project started and told them about Joshua. The name struck them immediately, and they asked numerous questions as to Joshua's identity, where he was from, what was his background, would they meet this man, and any number of other questions. Elie tried to answer as best he could, but he realized that even though he and Joshua were close, he did not feel free to say too much. That was up to Joshua himself. He did, however, explain that he had a strong feeling that Joshua would be showing up soon and would play a big role in their mission. He assured them they would certainly enjoy meeting him, as he was a very unusual person.

Moshe excused himself to cook the supper. "You're welcome to come in the kitchen and chat while I'm cooking. I think better when I'm cooking. I can also listen better." Elie followed him into the kitchen.

"That priest up in Ibillin is quite a fellow," Moshe commented as he grabbed a frying pan from the rack over the counter. "What is your strategy, Elie? You had better have a good one."

"It really isn't my strategy. I was sent to contact friends of my friends back home and alert them as to our plans. Others will be arriving soon to pull everything together. Hopefully Joshua will be with them, and then you can all discuss what you feel is the best course of action. My purpose basically is to test the waters. We felt it important to make sure our friends would be willing to make a concerted effort to pressure the antagonists to sit down and hammer out a peace agreement that will be approved and accepted by all parties. I know it sounds like an impossible dream, but since everything else has failed, why not get all the important people together and let the politicians know how much support there is for peace?"

"Well, you're right there. We have tried everything else. One last big push might be just what is needed, especially if we all get together on it. How will we know where to meet and when?"

"That will be announced as soon as I finish making contact

with all your important friends. I am surprised how many friends Ibrahim Abdul has not only in Arab countries, but even here in Israel."

"Yes, well, you have to understand, Ibrahim is a businessman and a very shrewd diplomat. His integrity is his badge of honor. Everyone who does business with him has learned to trust him. His involvement with this project injects confidence and hope into the high possibility of its success. I cannot imagine him embarking on a venture that would not ultimately be successful. He is too shrewd for that, so you should have no trouble rounding up his friends. Well, let's get ready for supper."

At supper and for a short time afterward, they continued discussing ideas and practical possible plans once things started rolling. As there was much to be done the following day, they retired early.

Next morning after breakfast, as Elie was leaving, the parting was sentimental. They had had such a good time the night before and felt so close to each other, not only in dreams, but in temperament and similar humor, that parting was difficult. They all had tears in their eyes as Elie pulled out of the driveway.

Elie's next stop was in Tel Aviv, where he was to meet another businessman. This person was recommended not only by Ibrahim, but by several contacts he had already met. This man was one of the wealthiest in Israel, having started a pharmaceutical company many years ago when the country was just getting on its feet. His interest in the peace movement was not necessarily motivated by the highest ideals; to him it was a commercial necessity. He did not want the country to have to depend on the United States for its survival. With Jewish expertise and Arab investments, a powerful economic bloc could revolutionize the whole Middle East for the better and raise the spirits of the entire area. Elie was looking forward to meeting this man.

He was not disappointed. Mikhael Avaron had emigrated with his family from Iran in the late forties, bringing his fortune with him in prudent increments and reestablishing his business in Israel, with corporate headquarters in Tel Aviv. His was one of the first high-tech businesses in the country and soon grew into a thriving multinational corporation. Having kept all his influential business contacts and an important factory in Tehran, he still had a strong foothold in a Muslim country, with the potential for expanding into surrounding Arab countries. This was his long-term dream. The plan Elie was promoting fit precisely into Avaron's business scheme, which he felt was good not only for *his* business, but for the economy of the whole region.

Elie received an enthusiastic welcome, as his visit was expected because of the priest's phone call.

"Mr. Avaron?" Elie questioned as the man came out the front door to meet him.

"Yes, that's me. And you are Mr. Zambaka. I recognize that name. I had good friends in Iran by that name."

"I am sure they are relatives. We used to live there ourselves until we left for the United States. I miss Iran. It is a beautiful country, and the people are so warm and sensitive."

"Come inside, my friend, come inside! I must tell you, I had a phone call just an hour ago from your friend Ibrahim and some of the others in your group. They will be here shortly. They are going to work with you and coordinate meetings with their contacts in Israel and among the Palestinians."

"Did they mention Joshua?"

"No. Who is he?"

"He is the one who dreamed up this whole idea. He's a genius, and a man who cares for people, all people. He is nonpolitical. I hope he is with them. His presence always makes me feel safe."

"I would like to meet him already. I do hope he comes. Now, may I offer you tea or coffee, or perhaps spirits?"

"Could I have a brandy?"

"Of course."

Mr. Avaron was a very proper and dignified gentleman of noble bearing. One could imagine him as a descendant of a long line of aristocrats. He was entirely different from Mr. Sharon, yet they were good friends. Elie felt a little uneasy with his new host, whose aristocratic manners were gracious and impeccable. Elie was just an easygoing, down-to-earth, warm human being with a most charming personality.

The two men wasted no time delving into the purpose of Elie's visit. Mr. Avaron had contacted Ibrahim personally and learned firsthand just what was about to take place, so he was already familiar with what Elie had to tell him. Elie's presence and manner of presenting the strategy convinced him there was a possibility it might just work.

It was not long before the others arrived from the airport. Elie and Mr. Avaron went out to welcome them. In the group were ten persons, among them Ibrahim; Rabbi Rapkin; elderly Mr. Greenberg and Brad Broyles from the rabbi's congregation; Norm Brickman, a synagogue trustee; and Rashid Abboud. As Rabbi Rapkin appeared, Mr. Avaron welcomed her with open arms and hugged her enthusiastically. They had been dear friends for years.

The last one to exit the taxi was Joshua. Elie could not hold his excitement.

"Am I glad to see you," he said as he ran and embraced him mightily, kissing him three times.

Joshua smiled broadly. He too was glad to see Elie. He loved him dearly and appreciated his generosity in fulfilling so willingly the not so nice assignment he had been given. He knew it had caused him many panic attacks.

Elie immediately introduced Joshua to his host, so excited was he for them to meet. He then apologized for almost ignoring the others. They could understand Elie's enthusiasm, because they shared what he was feeling about Joshua. Many things had happened after Elie left on his mission, things that made Joshua very much a part of their lives. Some of them also had the joy of meeting Joshua's mother and had come to realize the important role she had been playing in their lives and in the lives of many of their families. She had been quietly visiting several of the hurting families of those who were unjustly detained in holding pens for months on end as possible criminal suspects. She had been an angel of mercy, comforting and consoling especially the children of those families. It made no difference whether they were Muslims or Christians; they were still God's children and, more important, were innocent of any wrongdoing.

After the greetings and salutations, Mr. Avaron escorted everyone inside and set out a tray of cheese, olives, and salami and a bottle of wine, a pot of tea, and a pitcher of goat milk for his Muslim guests. They then plunged into a discussion of their planned strategy and of those important individuals who still needed to be contacted.

"Marsha, our friend Mordecai unfortunately will not be with us today," Mr. Avaron informed the group by way of addressing his rabbi friend. "He is meeting with the prime minister this very hour. In fact, he is discussing with him what we will be discussing today. Hopefully, the prime minister will listen with an open mind what he has to say. He is not an easy person to talk to about dialogue. He and Arafat are so poisoned against each other. But Sharon has great respect for Mordecai, and if anyone can get through to him, Mordecai is the one. He should have some news for us after his meeting. I expect he will be here by late supper."

"I will be happy to see him," Marsha responded. "It has been so long."

"Ibrahim," Mr. Avaron said, "this whole thing is going to be a gigantic undertaking in every way. I hope you realize we are all putting our lives on the line in becoming a part of this undertaking. Radicals on both sides will be inflamed at our concerted effort to demand a peaceful settlement. Even the assassination of prime ministers is within the realm of possibility."

"I realize that, Mikhael, but did not you and I risk our lives over much less important adventures than what we are attempting now? At least now it is not about business ventures, but the possibility of salvaging the peace of the world. That is not an unworthy cause to be willing to die for, if necessary. Besides, we have the clear assurance that this will be successful."

"All dreamers have a clear assurance of success, my friend," Mikhael retorted with a smile.

"Mikhael," Ibrahim said by way of moving the conversation forward, "do you have any suggestions as to how we should go about contacting others in the area? I think Joshua is interested in visiting those villages where Hamas and the Jihad are strong. I tried to tell him that that was dangerous, but he still feels it is important that he go there. The rest of us, I would think, should meet some of the peace activists, especially those from both sides who are working together."

"That is an excellent first step. They are well organized and can be of tremendous help. I would also suggest we contact some of the Israeli military leaders. Many of them of late are convinced that there can be no possible military solution to this mess and that only a political resolution can be really effective. I can be of some help in arranging meetings with them. We might also try to talk with members of the Likud and the Labor Party. That will at best bring a very mixed response. I can make arrangements with members of the Labor Party. I think it best if Mordecai makes arrangements with the Likud. That's not going to be an easy task."

"I would like to start out first thing tomorrow morning," Joshua interjected. "I will go to Nablus, Hebron, and Jennin and meet with as many of the people there who will listen."

"That will be a most dangerous undertaking, Joshua. Do be careful," Mikhael warned.

"I appreciate your concern, and I assure you, I will be most careful."

The day passed quickly. Riva Avaron, Mikhael's wife and Marsha Rapkin's dear friend, arrived just in time for supper. Joshua, who had insisted on cooking the meal, since cooking was a mystery to Mikhael, had supper all prepared when she arrived. The rest of the evening was more relaxing than business oriented.

CHAPTER

16

NEXT MORNING, JOSHUA WAS THE FIRST ONE UP. HE walked outside and drank in the fresh air floating in from across the Mediterranean. He was home again. It felt so good. His people, his land, all the memories of his life so long ago. He felt so happy and lighthearted in spite of the difficult mission ahead. Things had changed in twenty centuries, but things were also much the same. His people lived here again. He was happy about that, though sad that there was so little room to share.

After breakfast, he left to go to Nablus. Mikhael offered to have his chauffeur drive him, but Joshua insisted he would have no trouble arriving where he needed to be. He had his own ways. The others made arrangements to meet with their contacts. They invited Elias Chacour to come to Avaron's house for dinner the following evening so he and his Arab and Israeli friends would be included and play a significant role in the mission. They were determined to leave no stone unturned in an effort to gather together friends who could wield an over-whelming pressure on those whose consent was a necessity for any lasting peace accord.

Later that morning, Mikhael received an urgent phone call from a friend who learned that Mr. Sharon had been contacted by American intelligence and warned of dangerous terrorist suspects coming to Israel. They mentioned Elie, Joshua, Rabbi Rapkin, and other members of Ibrahim's group. Mikhael's friend was instructed to find out from him what this was all about, as his name was mentioned also as a possible contact, and then get back to the prime minister with the information. Mikhael laughed out loud and assured his friend it had to be a colossal misunderstanding, as these very people had been plan-ning a project for peace for many months and this was the cul-mination of all their hard work.

Joshua arrived in Nablus before noon and found himself in the middle of a crowd where everyone knew everyone else and he was a stranger. Who was he and what was he doing there?

As he walked down the street, two boys were playing. One tripped and fell, scraping his legs on the rough pavement. Joshua picked him up, brushed off his clothes, and dried the tears from his eyes.

"Be careful, little one, it is easy to get hurt when you play in crowds like this."

The boy thanked him and walked away with his playmate.

As a policeman approached, Joshua greeted him and asked if he would kindly show him the way to President Arafat's of-fice.

"Do you have an appointment, sir?"

"No, but I have something very important to discuss with him, and I know he will see me. Just tell him I come from Ibrahim Abdul and Mikhael Avaron. He will understand."

The compound, or what was left of it after the recent shelling by Israeli troops, was only two blocks away. Joshua followed the officer down the street and waited outside while the man entered the building with Joshua's message.

After a wait that seemed like an hour but was only fifteen minutes, two armed, crusty-looking men came out with the policeman and approached Joshua.

"What is your name?"

"Joshua."

"Why are you here?"

"I have been sent by Ibrahim Abdul and was told I would be expected and assured I would be given a warm welcome."

"What is the address and telephone number of Ibrahim Abdul?"

Joshua gave them the information they requested, and he was conducted into Chairman Arafat's sparse and poorly decorated quarters and offered a seat.

After a short wait, he was brought into the chairman's office and greeted warmly by Mr. Arafat.

"Joshua, you have come most highly recommended by my friend Ibrahim. I am sorry you were inconvenienced a few minutes ago, but we have to be so careful, as there are some who would like to see me eliminated. As a result, I have to be more cautious than usual."

"I understand. I am not offended."

"Please be seated, Joshua. Now tell me about this extraordinary mission that my friend and you have developed and which you are so impatient to share with us."

"As you are aware, Mr. Arafat, you have many friends and your people have many friends and relatives in the United States. They are all very much upset at seeing the most dedicated of their young people living here being sent off to destroy themselves. Young people so dedicated should be the hope of the future. Only the Evil One could inspire such a horrible nightmare, to destroy the youth of a people and bankrupt the future of the whole nation. I am sure you do not approve of this tactic, yet nothing effective has been done to stop it.

"Your friends back in the United States have decided to send delegations to all the important people on all sides of the conflict here to try to develop a reasonable plan that could be acceptable to everyone involved. On the surface, this might seem like an impossibility, especially as there are groups on both sides who will not rest until the other side is completely destroyed or driven from the land. But we have still decided to do the best we can to help them see that there is no hope of that ever happening, and if that attempt does not stop, it will destroy the people."

"Well, my friend, at least you are aware that your mission might not succeed."

"No, on the contrary, this plan will succeed."

"May I ask what gives you the assurance of that?"

"God."

"God, Allah! And you have no doubt?"

"None."

"I wish I could be as sure of my own plans and dreams. So often they turn into nightmares. Joshua, since I have such respect for my friend Ibrahim and he has helped our poor people here with food and medicines, I am willing to lend whatever support I can to help you. What is it I can do for you?"

"Would you call together the most important members of all the various factions, including the most radical among your people, so I can talk with them?"

"That will be difficult. Many of them think I am going soft and no longer listen to me. But I will try. They might at least be talked into coming to a meeting. It might take a few days, so do not think I have forgotten you if you do not hear from me right away. I am sure we will have no trouble contacting you."

"I am grateful for your generosity, Mr. Arafat. I expect you will be successful."

Joshua left and wandered through the streets of the town, observing the bombed-out buildings and the depressed looks on the faces of the people. Their blank stares told him they were people who had lost hope.

Walking down a side street, he reached a small grove of olive trees at the edge of town. There, resting on the huge root of one of the trees, he began to pray.

"Father, this time we cannot fail. These people have to come back to life. They have lost all hope. Mother, this is a mission where you can really be a mother to these desolate people. Find the families of good people and comfort them. Tell them I send you to them to give them hope and courage not to abandon their dreams. Peace will come soon, and their children will again laugh with loud sounds of joy that will resound through the streets."

After his rest, Joshua returned to the main street, and as he walked along, he looked at each person he met and smiled. His look penetrated deep into their hearts; each one knew it, and as they moved on it was with a spark of hope, a miracle of a different kind. Farther down the street, he approached a little girl with one good arm and the other a mere stump. She had lost a hand. She walked with a limp. Joshua bent to talk to her. At first she was frightened, but after looking into his eyes, the fear left her.

"Little one, my Father made you to be happy and enjoy your life. Be healed and be happy from now on, and know that

God loves you very much." With that he rested his hand on her head and then walked on.

At first the girl noticed nothing; then all of a sudden she started screaming when she noticed that she had her hand again and could walk without a limp. "I am healed, I am healed!" she screamed as she ran down the street toward her home.

When she arrived at what was left of their house, she went inside. Her mother panicked when she heard the screams, ran to her, and immediately noticed her daughter had two hands and that she was not limping.

"Rebecca, Rebecca, what happened? How did all this happen, child?"

The little girl was so excited that she could barely tell her mother the story. Finally, she was able to stammer, "A man, a stranger walking down the street . . . He rested his hand on my head . . . and told me . . . told me God wanted me to be happy. Then he kept walking."

"Who was he?"

"I don't know, Mother. I never saw him before."

"What did he look like?"

"I don't know. He just had very kind eyes."

"Would you recognize him if you saw him again?"

"Oh, yes, Mother, I will never forget him. He has a beautiful face, not hard and angry like most men, but gentle and kind."

"We must find him and thank him."

By this time, Joshua was in another part of town in an isolated section off from the flow of traffic. Several men were sitting in a circle under a large olive tree, smoking water pipes and talking politics. Joshua stopped and greeted them in Arabic. They did not even bother to look up and in their surly, boorish manner let him know they were not interested in striking up a conversation. Joshua knew he would be unwelcome, because he knew who they were: angry people with strong radical leanings. They were part of the groups that encouraged suicide bombings and other murders of innocent people.

Undeterred by their boorish behavior, Joshua sat near them and said nothing for the longest time.

"Can't you tell you're not welcome, fellow? Get out of here and leave us alone."

"Many years ago, a people possessed by devils said the same thing to me: 'Leave us alone, we know who you are, the anointed of God.' "

"Are you telling us we are possessed by devils?"

"You are saying that. Those who do the work of the devil are possessed by the devil. If you do the work of the devil, then it is your works that betray you. God is a God of love. Those who love God do the work of God, and their goodness to others bears witness to God. Satan as the father of evil is devoid of love. His followers do not know love, and spread only murder and hatred, and destroy even their own children."

When the men heard that they wanted to tear Joshua apart, but there was something about his manner that transfixed them, and they did not dare even to move. Looking up from their pipes, they fixed their eyes on him in an attempt to read him and his strange behavior.

"Who are you?" one man asked.

"Where are you from?" another asked. "You are not from around here."

"What are you doing here?"

"I am Y'shua."

The men were shocked. They knew what that name meant, even though they were Muslims.

"What do you want with us?"

"I do not come to you because you are evil. I come to you because of the goodness that you have all but killed within you. I know you. I know you are men without hope, and in your desperation you strike out to destroy even the lives of your own children."

Struck by the blunt revelation of what they thought were their secret crimes, they felt as if their very souls had been stripped naked, and by a total stranger who did not even know them. They were speechless.

Then, coming to their senses, one of them rudely asked Joshua, "All right, what do you want with us?"

"The total conversion of your hearts to God."

"You're crazy, fellow."

"I tell you solemnly, before this year ends, you will find yourselves in the depths of hell if you do not repent. You convince your sons that they are martyrs if they die while killing innocent people, thereby sending your own children not to heaven, but to the brink of hell. It is only God's compassion that snatches their deceived and tortured souls from the clutches of Satan, and washes away the stains of your poison, and heals them of your evil."

Joshua got up from where he was sitting and walked away, leaving the men to their dark thoughts.

As soon as he left, a mother and child hurried frantically down the street and turned up the road to where the men were.

"Did you see a man pass by here?" the mother asked excitedly.

The men turned and eyed the woman suspiciously. Two of them knew her and her family.

"What happened to Rebecca?" one of them asked. "She has her hand back, and she can run."

"A man just healed her and we are trying to find him to thank him. Old Jezabel said he came up this street just a few minutes ago."

"What did he look like?"

"What did he look like, Rebecca?"

"I don't know, Mother. But I would recognize him if I saw him. His face was kind, and his hair was neat, but not long. He wore brown pants and a light brown shirt, open at the neck. That's all I know. But I don't know what he looks like."

The men were shaken. One of them told the woman, "That man was just here, but he left."

"Where did he go?" the mother asked.

"I don't know. He just walked back down the street. Can't be far from here. He just left."

"Thank you, thank you," she said in trembling voice. "The man must be from God. He healed my Rebecca. He gave her back her hand. I hope I can find him to thank him. He has been sent by Allah."

The men's dark, evil thoughts turned to fear. "He gave the girl back her hand. The woman said he's from Allah. He said his name was Y'shua, Jesus. This is crazy. No one gets a hand back. I'm going home."

The group broke up and all went to their homes, shaken.

The woman and child kept looking, but Joshua was nowhere to be found.

Around the same time, in another part of town, an old woman who had lost two sons and three grandchildren, and whose husband had died years before, was sitting in a dilapidated rocking chair. In her lonely despair, she was crying and pleading with God to take back her life. She could no longer stand the pain and the dreadful loneliness. Sensing the presence of someone nearby, she wiped the tears from her eyes and looked up to find a beautiful woman kneeling before her and looking with compassion into her eyes.

Frightened for a moment, she said to the visitor, "Who are you? What do you want of me?"

"Susanna, I am Miriam. I want nothing of you. I came to be a comfort to you."

"Who are you and how do you know me? I am a stranger to you."

"My son sent me to be your friend and to comfort you in your loneliness."

"Who is your son?"

"My son is Y'shua."

"Y'shua? And your name is Miriam. But do you not know that I am Muslim?"

"I know, and I know that even though you know me only from your Koran, you have been talking to me in your loneliness and I have prayed for you. That is why my son wanted me to visit you and become your friend."

"O Miriam, Miriam. Dear Mother, how I have learned to love you through the years. Your life was lonely like mine, and I could feel your pain at seeing your son suffer so much. I knew you would understand my sorrow. And you did. Thank you, thank you so much for coming to me. You have lifted a heavy burden from my heart. I can live again. Please visit me again. You mean so much to me."

"I will visit you again, Susanna. I will leave now, but know that I will never be far away. Be at peace, and know that my son loves you and has died for you, too. So one day you will be with him in paradise, and with your children, too."

"Please don't go yet. Please let me cook for you a bowl of soup, so we can eat together. I would be so honored to share with you what little I have."

Miriam smiled and helped the old lady from her chair and walked with her into the kitchen, where the old woman cooked their meager meal. As they sat and sipped their soup and ate their crusts of bread, Susanna reached out and took Miriam's hand and pressed it to her lips, kissing it tenderly as the tears flowed down her wrinkled cheeks.

"I love you, dear Mother. I love you, and I love your son, too. I always have, even though I could never share it with anyone."

"I know, and I love you, too. You are very dear to me."

After eating their meal, Miriam kissed the woman on both cheeks and walked into another world.

The woman slept soundly and peacefully that night for the first time in many years, dreaming beautiful dreams of her new friend.

THE REST OF THAT DAY JOSHUA SPENT VISITING OTHER members of radical groups, meeting them in odd places where he could catch them off guard and in no position to be obnoxious toward him. All he wanted to do was communicate to them much the same message he had delivered to the first group he met, that the work they were doing was not the work of a loving God, but the work of the devil, delivering their own children into the hands of Satan.

The message did not sit well with them, nor was it long before they all met up with members of the first group, who had met the woman whose daughter was healed by Joshua. They ended up having totally mixed-up feelings, anger, confusion, guilt over what they might have done to their children if this stranger was right. The more the men talked about what Joshua had said, even after they learned of his healing the young girl, the angrier they became toward him for stirring up their consciences, which they all had deadened so carefully.

Joshua knew this would happen. It happened the same way in the old days. Exposing people's evil ways did not endear him to them but drove them to hate him all the more. This time he had another plan, however, which would turn out to be most effective, and it was executed on a Friday evening when Mr. Arafat managed to gather together leaders of Hamas, Hezbollah, and other activist groups at a service held in a mosque in a quieter part of town. After the service, which Joshua attended, the leaders retired to a large meeting room. Mr. Arafat did not attend. His presence anywhere was always monitored and would have been an unnecessary giveaway that something important was afoot. But there was one stranger at the mosque service who walked in with Joshua and also retired with him to the meeting room.

As the meeting started, not everyone knew one another, so introductions became a necessity. They knew of Joshua's presence, though they had not met him. And they were all curious as to the identity of the person with him.

Mr. Arafat's representative chaired the meeting and initiated the introductions. When he arrived at the man with Joshua, he asked his name and what group he was with. The man merely replied, "My name is Muhammad."

"Muhammad what?" asked the chairman.

"Muhammad. That is my name. I have no other."

"What group are you with?"

"I am from Mecca, of the tribe of Fihr, Quraish."

"Never heard of it."

"Those who know their holy book know of what I speak. I am here this evening because Joshua asked me to be with him when he spoke with you, feeling that I might be a help to him."

Seeing that the man was with Joshua, for whom the meeting was called, the chairman ended his interrogation. Even though the chairman was not very familiar with his religion, some of the others listening were well acquainted with their religion and their sacred writings and were filled with curiosity, dying to know more about this man. They knew the prophet Muhammad had been born in Mecca. They knew he belonged to the tribe of Fihr, or Quraish, as it was sometimes called. Some Muslim writers wrote detailed descriptions of Muhammad, even to the kind of clothing he wore. This man fitted their descriptions perfectly. So they were very curious. Either this man was a nut or they were experiencing a profound supernatural phenomenon.

After all the introductions and greetings, the chairman introduced Joshua and invited him to address the group.

"My name is Joshua. I come to you from a group of your American relatives and friends who are deeply saddened over the plight of their families here. They are troubled at the anguish of their loved ones here who have been reduced to such degrading conditions and despair. They have long come to the conclusion that conditions cannot be resolved by endless military struggle. Only calm heads and reason can prevail. They are also appalled at seeing the best of their young people destroying their own lives, thinking they will save their people in this way. As a result, many of us formed a large organization composed of Jews and Arabs in America who have vast contacts and influence in these parts, to exercise that influence to foster peace in this holy but troubled land. It has been appointed for me to speak with you. Some of the others are meeting with Israeli military and political leaders, hoping to help them see that there can be no possible military solution to this problem. Continued hatred has no happy ending, because retaliation always demands the last act of revenge.

"Precise and detailed plans for peace have already been proposed. Our intention in speaking to you this evening is to convince you to take the right step and, out of love for your children and grandchildren, give peace a chance. Even if some hostile acts are committed by the other side, let them pass. We will put extreme pressure on them also to desist from hostile action against your people. Things may not be perfect in the beginning, but time will work in your favor and, in truth, in everyone's favor. Hatred must end. Give your leaders a chance to work out the details of a peace agreement that will be acceptable to both sides, so you can live side by side and slowly heal wounds that have festered for too long. In this way you can have much of your land back and you can start to build a healthy, free society with a strong economy, where your children can grow and learn how to live happy, fulfilled lives."

From the back of the room, a deep angry voice spoke up. "Who are you to come into our village and tell us what we must do to find peace? You have never suffered injustice and degradation the way we have here, and you dare to tell us what we must do? We know what we must do. We must drive every damn Jew out of our country. They have seized it from us. We have been treated like you people treated the Indians in your country. You have destroyed them, destroyed their dignity, their honor, their pride. Now two hundred years later they still live in degradation because they trusted you and tried to make peace with you. Well, that's not going to happen here. We will not rest until we drive every Jew out of our land."

There was a boisterous expression of applause and agreement when the man finished his speech. Others took their turns endorsing the position.

Joshua realized the depth and extent of their frustration and despair. He let them speak and did not contradict them. When they finished their expressions of agreement, he spoke.

"It is not easy for me to speak to you tonight. I know I have not lived through your experiences, but I can see very clearly that given the vast imbalance of arms and military resources, you cannot win a military victory. You will all be slowly destroyed until there is nothing left. By giving peace a chance, you will have a good portion of your land back and a chance to build up your nation and provide healthy, normal lives for your people, if your people is what really concerns you. If personal vengeance is your real concern, then you have chosen to destroy the future of your own families and your whole nation. The choice is yours."

No matter what Joshua said, no one seemed willing to break ranks and agree with him. In fact, things were turning sour, and some speakers started openly to insult him.

At that point, Muhammad spoke up. "I will speak to you bluntly. You people are not my disciples. You use your religion to justify your evil deeds. Where in the Koran have I ever told my followers that they should send out little children to destroy themselves as suicide bombers? I tell you to your faces, you are cowards. I see that none of you had the courage to go out and blow yourselves up. But you have the heartlessness to tell your own children to do so, having convinced them that they would go to heaven for doing something that I forbade in my holy book. I tell you, you are not religious men. You are evil men. You may go through the motions of religious practice, but in your hearts you neither fear Allah nor care for what He commands. Joshua, Jesus, who stands at my side, is right, and if you do not listen to him and repent, I tell you, it will not go well with you after death, when you appear before him as your judge, as is written in the holy book."

When Muhammad finished there was an eerie silence throughout the whole room. No one could believe what was appearing to take place before their very eyes, Muhammad, Jesus. Finally, an old man spoke up. "Sir, if you are Muhammad, the founder of our religion, give us some proof that it is really you."

"You are a religious man. You have read the holy books and books about my life. Come up here to me."

As the man stood before Muhammad, the Prophet said to him, "You know the kind of clothes I wore. What were they like?"

"Just like the clothes you are wearing now."

"When my followers attacked Mecca, I received a slight wound. You have read about all the details of my life in my biographies, so you should know the place of that wound. Find it."

The old man was at first reluctant to handle the Prophet, if indeed that was who it was, but he timidly pushed back the loose sleeve covering the Prophet's right arm. On the underside of his arm just below the elbow was the two-inch-long scar.

"Holy Prophet, forgive me. I believe now. I know it is you."

Muhammad embraced the old man and praised him for his goodness, and the honesty of his life, and his dedication to Allah.

Though the old man's heart changed in that moment, the rest of the crowd was still undeterred. Hatred does not leave a tortured soul that easily. One man expressed what some others felt, even though to a religious Muslim it was blasphemy: "If that is what Muhammad teaches, then I am no longer a Muslim. Even he is out of touch with our life here." He got up and walked out, while muttering for everyone to hear, "If hell is what I must pay to drive the Jews out of our land, then hell is where I will go."

The rest of the group were shaken, some with confusion, some with guilty hearts, some, though now not many, feeling that they too might end damned to hell.

Before the meeting broke up, Mr. Arafat made a brief appearance. He had witnessed what had just taken place and was shaken when he realized the presence of Muhammad, and that Joshua was Jesus. He knew the evening would be difficult, as he had had dealings with these people many times. There was no way of talking sense to them; their hatred and need for vengeance were too deep. Some even considered him a traitor when he tried to discuss terms of peace, though at his appearance everyone still stood up to welcome him.

He spoke briefly. "I want to thank you for coming here tonight. I cannot stay long. I have to move quickly. What these two holy men have proposed tonight, I only ask you to take to heart. Our options are very few, and our only aim should be how best we can salvage the lives and dignity of our people. Satisfying personal hatred and need for revenge can no longer be an option if we are truly interested in the future of our people. That is all I have to say. Good night, and may Allah protect us and preserve our people."

Then he walked over to Muhammad and Joshua, bowed his head deeply to both of them, and begged their blessing. Looking at Joshua, he said humbly, "I celebrate your birthday each year at Mass in Bethlehem. Your message of forgiveness has touched me only too late. You go many steps beyond what we were taught."

Muhammad nodded in agreement. "The law of retribution is not godly, as we had all thought," he said. "It invalidates God's command to love as He loves and to forgive as He forgives us. We say 'God is merciful and forgiving,' but we do not practice what he tells us."

"Only too late have I learned," Mr. Arafat said, then walked out of the room.

As the meeting came to an end, only a few people came up to talk to Joshua and Muhammad. They expressed how much they were struggling with the issues they spoke about. Joshua told them it was not easy, but with prayer God would give them the grace to do the right thing.

During this time Miriam had been busy, visiting the homes of some of the men who were at the meeting. Those families were most troubled, with mothers and young brothers and sisters grieving for a brave brother who had been pressured into becoming a suicide bomber.

Comforting them was not entirely possible, as the women did not share their fanatic husbands' belief that the children would be looked upon as martyrs by Allah. Miriam could only assure them that in spite of what they had done, God was compassionate and understood that the dead children were victims of loyalty to a father's misguided sense of what would please God. They could count on God's forgiveness because they had not known. In each of the homes, Miriam accepted the hospitality offered by having a little something to eat with them, even if it was only a crust of bread and a cup of tea. When they were finally convinced Miriam was Jesus' mother, the honor they felt was a great comfort in the realization that God had indeed blessed them. Later on, when their husbands returned home from the meeting, the wives shared the story of Miriam's visit; and after they heard what their wives told them, their consciences were more troubled than ever. For the men, that night was filled with tortured, sleepless dreams. The women and children, however, slept peacefully for the first time in many nights.

IBRAHIM AND THE OTHER MEMBERS OF THE MISSION HAD met with Elias Chacour. He was beside himself with joy that something was finally being done on a scale that had the potential for success. He was only too familiar with all the previous failed attempts at peace. This one seemed to be organized widely enough and with the right persons involved to make sense. Using all Ibrahim's personal contacts in Jerusalem and among Israeli Arabs in the government, plus the American groups' contacts, the mission members literally blitzed the top government officials and businesspeople.

Many members of the Labor Party were most willing to cooperate. Even a good number of Likud were willing to listen, though some were adamantly opposed and refused to meet with the group. Radical right-wing groups turned a deaf ear. They were already too scared that even their former erstwhile hero Sharon was beginning to turn traitor to his former sacred commitments and was starting to dismantle settlements on the

West Bank. They were beginning to feel doomed and refused to consider any talk of peace, because peace meant compromise, and compromise meant giving away land, which most likely meant a part of Jerusalem itself. A great fear looming in their nightmares was the high birthrate among Arabs, which if they had their own state would explode way beyond the population of Israel.

The businessmen in the mission won the day with moderate leaders and even moderate-leaning radicals. Elie's quiet groundbreaking work over the past weeks had produced commitments guaranteeing that if the Israelis were generous enough in a peace settlement with the Palestinians, businesses in their own countries would establish financial and business ties with Israel and in time work to form their own economic bloc in the Middle East. This was not a pipe dream. It was an economic necessity if any of the countries in the Middle East were to survive economically. The ongoing Palestinian-Israeli conflict had paralyzed the whole region for decades and was destroying all their economies. Working together was the only medicine, as bitter as it might be initially, for a return to economic health.

While intensive meetings were being held in a dozen places around Israel, a cipher had surfaced in the project. Ever since Elie had left Syria for Damascus, his movements had been carefully watched, with spies passing on information to every place he went. Elie himself was unaware of this, though ever since the explosion on the road to Damascus, he knew there were people who were very unhappy with what he was doing. Fear of some impending danger never left him. The only time he felt safe was when Joshua was nearby. And Joshua was not very nearby.

In fact, Joshua was busy meeting with Mr. Arafat at that very moment. Arafat had been impressed since their first brief meeting. Though he was tilting toward peace, he was more afraid of his own radicals than he was of the Israelis. He knew most of the Israeli people wanted peace, and their own radicals were tame in comparison with his own opposition groups. Joshua's coming, however, changed everything; he persuaded Mr. Arafat to meet with the Israelis and come to a final peace settlement. Though he had waffled before at critical points, he was now strong enough to make a personal commitment to Joshua, especially after what he had experienced at the previous night's meeting.

The commitment he made to Joshua at this meeting he was determined to keep, even though he was fearful of possible consequences to himself. After paying Joshua gestures of deepest respect, since he now knew who he really was, he thanked him profusely and had his own guards escort him safely from the village.

Joshua then returned to Jerusalem, and it was none too soon. It was almost as if he knew he had to be there. As he approached the building where Ibrahim and Mikhael and the others were meeting with Mr. Sharon, he had to walk past a huge crowd of people, Israelis and Arabs, chanting peace slogans. They were the peace group that had been working for years with Elias Chacour. He had arranged for them to be there during this critical meeting with the prime minister, to apply as much pressure as possible outside while they were negotiating with him inside.

When Joshua was ushered into the meeting, he was welcomed by his friends and introduced to Mr. Sharon, who was most gracious toward him. Mikhael informed him that it was Joshua who had conceived the whole idea of bringing everyone together from all sides in one final attempt to make peace. The prime minister resented having to act under such extreme pressure, but he was of course familiar with pressure of all kinds. The latest, still ongoing, was pressure from the military commanders who were sick of a dirty war that stripped them of their dignity and pride as professional soldiers. What Sharon had forced them to do in Arab villages was demeaning to their sense of pride and troubling to their consciences, and more and more of their ranks were resenting it. So the timing of this meeting with Joshua's group was most fortuitous. Everything was coming together nicely.

The real clincher, which was the fruit of Elie's hard work over the past weeks, was a commitment to the prime minister from the heads of neighboring Arab states to be willing to establish diplomatic relations with Israel if the government was generous in its peace agreement with the Palestinians. They also offered to negotiate lucrative trade agreements with Israel that would be a boon to Israel's sagging economy as well as to their own. Before the meeting ended, Mr. Sharon agreed to meet with Mr. Arafat's representatives. He could not yet agree to meet with Arafat personally; his hatred for the man was too deep. But he still agreed to work out a final settlement with Arafat's representatives.

The meeting ended with spontaneous expressions of joy from everyone. Walking out of the building and into the crowd, which was still chanting loudly, the whole group burst into wild applause at having attained their goal. Everyone hugged and kissed one another and broke down crying with joy.

In all the excitement, Elie, who was standing with Joshua, fell to the pavement. Gradually the whole crowd grew silent. Joshua knelt and lifted Elie's head onto his lap. Blood was streaming from Elie's chest. He had been shot, though no one had heard the sound.

"Joshua, I am going to die, aren't I. You can heal me if you want, I know. But to die in your arms is the greatest joy I can think of, so I won't even ask you to heal me. I look forward to being with my mother and to being forever with you. I am sorry if I was not always the kind of person you would have liked me to be, but I tried so hard, and you know how much I love you. Please forgive me for my failings."

"Elie, you have always been a beautiful person, with a kind and generous heart. What happened here today would not be as perfect as it was had you not worked so hard to do your part. Your failings in life, as many as they may have been, are forgiven because you have loved much. This day, my dear friend, you will be with me in paradise. May the angels receive you into my home and your mother greet you on your way."

With that Joshua pressed him to his heart and Elie died in his arms. Tears streamed down Joshua's cheeks as he held the dead body against his breast.

Mr. Sharon, who had sensed something terrible had happened, came down to the group and heard every word of what transpired between Joshua and Elie.

"What happened? Who did it?"

Joshua looked up into Mr. Sharon's eyes and merely said, "Someone who does not want peace to succeed. It makes no difference who did it."

"This is what makes peace impossible," the prime minister retorted angrily.

"No, that is only a convenient excuse leaders use when they really do not want peace. Assassins must not be allowed to succeed. Peace must triumph over their evil."

Mr. Sharon looked at Ibrahim and asked, "Who is that man?"

Ibrahim looked into his eyes and replied, "It is Jesus. Did

you not hear what he said to the dying man—'This day you will be with me in paradise'?"

As emergency people arrived and lifted Elie's dead body onto the stretcher, the prime minister helped Joshua up from the pavement. As he rose, Joshua looked into the prime minister's eyes and said in a low voice that only he could hear, "You have witnessed today a mystery. Let its message bring peace to your troubled heart and strengthen your resolve to follow my Father's light."

The prime minister said nothing, but he was touched by the tenderness with which the words were spoken. It gave him much to ponder. He knew one thing it meant was that peace would finally take place and that he would be the instrument of Yahweh.

The following weeks were busy as both sides worked hard to make sure that this time peace would happen and their two peoples could finally live in harmony and security.

Unfortunately, when word spread that an accord was a likely possibility, all those threatened by the prospect of an imminent peace became unhinged. The unstable radicals on both sides fanned the embers of a general chaos. The Likud Party members did nothing to discourage the instability. Assassination attempts were made in Palestinian territories as well as in Jerusalem. One Israeli army general who was known to favor a peaceful settlement was seriously wounded in an assassination attempt. An attempt was even made on the life of Mr. Sharon. Mr. Arafat was fearful that some of his own radicals would try to kill him. He became more reclusive than ever, shutting himself up in a secret hideaway with his closest collaborators as they prepared documents for the meetings with Mr. Sharon.

Mr. Sharon showed that he was a real patriot. Even though

he had done downright evil things in the past and built settlements throughout Palestinian territory to frustrate any possible viable Palestinian state, he was now determined to do the right thing and insist upon their dismantlement. Though it was neither practicable nor feasible to bring the hundreds of thousands of refugees back into Israel, honest provisions were being considered to compensate them for the homes and property that had been taken from them.

As the day approached when the two teams of leading negotiators were to meet and hammer out the solid agreement, word leaked out and violence erupted in Palestinian territory as well as in major Israeli cities. The crisis become so frightening that arrangements had to be made for the meetings to take place in a neutral foreign country.

In the middle of the night, both parties took secret flights to Oslo, Norway; there the Norwegian government made a hideaway available to them where they could work in a peaceful and secure atmosphere.

Ten days later, after working sometimes for eighteen hours a day, they had a reasonable agreement that offered justice and security to both sides. The settlement was celebrated by a party thrown by the king of Norway for all the negotiators. No one ever would have thought that men who had spent their whole lives hating one another could have fun together at a party. But the pride they felt in what they had accomplished for their people, and the fact that they could agree to terms that had been so difficult to arrive at, brought them closer to one another, at least close enough so they could enjoy celebrating together.

For the time they had been in Norway, no one knew where they were. Reporters tried in vain to track them down. Members of the government had no idea what had happened or where they were until their plane touched down in Tel Aviv and a military escort brought the Israelis back to Jerusalem and the Palestinians back to Nablus.

The next step would be the hardest, approval by the Knesset for the Israelis and by the Palestinian Authority for the Palestinians. If they disapproved, it would all come to naught, a total waste of time. As the Likud threatened a walkout that would close down the government, and some of the radical terrorists in Palestinian territory threatened violence to elected Palestinian officials, an amazing thing happened.

Mr. Sharon decided to bypass the Knesset and bring the major details of the settlement directly to the people. After discussing it with Mr. Arafat and obtaining his approval, he published the agreement in the national newspapers for the people's approval.

It turned out to be a stroke of genius. The vast majority of people on both sides desperately wanted peace. They also knew that the radicals would do all in their power to prevent peace from happening, so when Mr. Sharon went directly to the people and asked for their consent publicly, the next day hundreds of thousands of people paraded through the streets of all the cities and towns across Israel, shouting and singing their approval. In the face of such universal approval, even those most violently opposed realized it was useless to resist any further.

The same thing happened throughout the Palestinian territory. Huge crowds of people poured into the streets screaming their applause, thus assuring Palestinian approval.

The date was set for the signing of the accord. It was decided to have the signing on the Temple Mount, in the middle of the vast plaza. The officials knew they were taking a big risk in having the signing in the open and at such a public place, but they felt it would give the people of both nations a chance to celebrate together.

When that day finally arrived, even a space as vast as the Mount was not large enough to accommodate the crowds. The ceremony was simple enough, with only a few speakers proclaiming the historic importance of the moment and asking the God of Abraham, whom both peoples worshipped, for blessing and guidance for the future of both their nations. Then, when Mr. Sharon and Mr. Arafat signed the accord, the crowd broke into wild applause, which temporarily drowned out the orchestras playing music that had been composed especially for the occasion.

Even though under ordinary circumstances such loud outbursts might have been considered sacrilegious considering the proximity of the sacred shrines, no one thought this exuberance out of place. Everyone felt it a joyful noise that went up to heaven as a prayer, a pleasing expression of their recognition of each other as the children of their heavenly Father, as well as children of their father Abraham, estranged from each other for centuries.

If, as Jesus said, "there is more rejoicing in heaven over one sinner repenting than over the ninety-nine just who need no repentance," then this joyful celebration must have reverberated with a million times more happiness in heaven than one could ever imagine. For Yahweh, Allah, to look down and see His children finally celebrating together brought more joy to God's heart than could ever be imagined.

The historic event was, naturally, televised worldwide. It was on the news all day in the United States. The two agents who had been tracking Joshua for all that time could not believe what they were seeing on the TV screen. Tom Clark said to his partner, "Well, I guess that man Joshua took us for a good ride, Dan. Who would have ever dreamed that all that time, that simple man and his friends were planning something as world-shaking as this, and right under our eyes?"

"How could someone so innocent appear so evil?" Tom wondered out loud.

"Perhaps because evil is in the mind of the one who sees goodness as evil," his partner retorted.

© Chris Kahley

ABOUT THE AUTHOR

JOSEPH F. GIRZONE retired from the active priesthood in 1981 and embarked on a second career as a writer and speaker. In 1995 he established the Joshua Foundation, an organization dedicated to making Jesus better known throughout the world. His bestselling books include *Joshua*, *A Portrait of Jesus*, and *Never Alone*. He lives in Altamont, New York.